GOING HOME
FOR
APPLES
AND OTHER
STORIES

GOING HOME FOR APPLES AND OTHER STORIES

Richard Michael O'Meara

ISBN: 1508920494
ISBN 13: 9781508920496
Library of Congress Control Number: 2015904322
CreateSpace Independent Publishing Platform
North Charleston, South Carolina

ACKNOWLEDGMENTS

This work is affectionately dedicated to soldiers, one and all, who show up and do their jobs, in spite of their youth and the extraordinary chaos about them; and to Mary, who always gives me someone special to come home to.

November 2014

FOR A SOLDIER

Remember him,
For he is brighter than the mistletoe
You use to mark your door
This Christmas.
Remember him,
For, if he could,
His gaze would reach across the shores
And melt into your heart.
Remember him,
For he is lost
And left behind in jungles still,
Weary for the seasons past,
As you have lived beyond him.
He is a prayer of sorts,
A burning piece of incense,
A memory forgotten.
Remember him.

TABLE OF CONTENTS

GOING HOME FOR APPLES

In all the fall seasons that have passed, as I have tucked myself into bed contemplating the pending frost and the grandness of the moon, with all that I have forgotten and dropped along the way, my last thoughts each night are of Danny Joy and his apples. He has been as a shadow these forty-odd years, gone in the summer months, frozen and forgotten in wintertime and spring. Yet he returns in late September, just as the sun goes down and the chill stretches over the trees. I am not sure why he comes back each year, but I am sure that if one fall season he fails to appear, it will be time for me to die.

Fort Dix, New Jersey, in July is a terrible place to learn to do sit-ups, run innumerable miles through the sand, and stand long hours in the rain. That was especially true in 1967, when Danny and I first met. We sat cramped in the back of a long green bus crammed with other young men standing, sitting, and holding on for dear life, as the bus careened around turns, taking us from the staging area to our basic training company. We had all been shorn of our hair and everything else that was personal to us. Except for the large duffel bags, which kept us from bouncing against the wall of the bus, we had nothing to hold on to. And we knew it. Status was important though. We had been told that we weren't privates yet, not even soldiers, but no longer civilians. Instead, we were something in between. But even then, some were more important than others. A kid in the front, for example, had two stripes taped to his sleeve. He had been in the army a week longer than us, and therefore was in charge of the bus. We listened to everything he had to say, when we could. But in the back of the bus, where the draftees were made to sit, we couldn't hear much.

I stared at Danny's ass as we traveled. I could tell he was tall, even as I sat on the floor on my bag. In fact, his legs seemed to stretch clear to the rafters. He had the same baggy fatigue pants we all wore, but his seemed to fit somehow; I wondered why he had been issued the right clothes while mine appeared to belong to someone else, someone infinitely larger. He didn't seem to be sweating, either, which began to piss me off. How was it in a bus full of scared teenage boys, in ninety-five-degree weather, bags and bodies packed like pressed fish parts top to bottom, Danny stood holding on to a strap, smiling, cool as can be? It wasn't natural, and it sure wasn't normal.

"Look at that!" he exclaimed to no one in particular. "A tank. Look, there's a tank!" Everybody above me stretched to look out one of the windows, leaning on the bottom dwellers.

"Heh!" I yelled. "Get off my goddamn leg." The tank went by, and the mass of bodies swayed back toward the front of the bus. I felt like I was going to suffocate and tried to space the bus out. Someone farted, and all the draftees in the back began to giggle and moan. "Be there soon," Danny said into the neck of the man next to him. "Be there real soon!"

And that would not be the last time Danny proved prophetic. First, a right turn into a parking lot, all bodies swaying, and then a quick left straightening out, then a sudden stop. Bags and bodies tumbling, curses flying. "Ass over tea kettle" as the army was fond of saying. And us just learning the lingo. "Seems like the driver is just as new as we are," Danny mumbled, pulling himself erect. And, of course, that is when the firestorm began. A big corporal, with Smokey-the-Bear hat and sunglasses covering his eyes, walked up the stairs of the bus and started screaming.

"Ged off this goddamn bus, you pieces of shit! Ged off this bus before I come back there 'n' kick the lily-white off you little baby girls! Ged off this bus! Gedt, get! Get!" With that, the big hat with the voice and no eyes reached out and grabbed the first person in a seat, a large black kid named O'Neal, and with one hand pulled him to the stairs and pushed him off the bus head first onto the tarmac. "Soul brother thinks he's my friend. Thinks we like the same music. Thinks we brothers! Hah! That dopey bastard's gonna be the first one to recycle even if he is in the National Guard. Gotta get through me before you get to go home 'n' hide. Now gedt! Get off this fuckin' bus!"

"That's the scariest son of a bitch I've ever seen." The words dribbled out of Danny's mouth and landed around me on the floor. "Sure hope he gets tired sometimes." So we started running, each guy in the back running over me, and me unable to get up. Each heading for the door, scared to leave the bus but more scared to stay inside. That's when Danny reached down and grabbed me up.

"Looks like it's time to go," he says and starts running. When he hits the doorway, he takes a look outside into the bright sun and trips on the stairs. His bag falls…He falls. They both land on the hot blacktop in a pile surrounded by four other hats—big men with sticks and bulging chests, all screaming, gesturing with their arms and looking like Danny was personally insulting their mothers.

"Gedt up! Gedt up! Gedt up, you lazy sonofabitch! You think we got time to let you sleep! Charlie sees you sleepin' he'll sneak up 'n' cut your dick off. Now get your shit 'n' stand in that line. Stand! Stand! Stand up! Recover, you lanky bastard! 'N' take that shit-eatin' grin off your face!" I couldn't see it because I was still standing at the top of the stairs, but I guessed Danny was grinning that grin he always gets when he's nervous. "You think this shit's funny, you dumb fuck? You think I'm funnin' with you?" Now all the hats were around Danny, yelling down at him as he struggled to get up.

"'N' what the fuck is you lookin' at?" One of the hats noticed me still standing at the head of the stairs watching them all screaming at

Danny. "Geddoff that fuckin' bus now!" the hat screamed. And down I came, blinded by the sun and falling over Danny's bag on top of him. Immediately the other kids, lined up and standing at what they thought was the position of attention, started laughing, some howling in glee at the scene.

"You men, shut the fuck up!" the corporal yelled, leaving Danny and me and striding over to the line. The hat's neck seemed to stretch an extra five inches, as he put his face directly into the face of one of the guys standing in line. "You think this shit is funny? You think it's a fuckin' joke when one of your men falls down 'n' gets wounded? Why I wouldn't TAKE your sorry ass to the Nam. No sir! You too fuckin' dangerous. I think I'm gonna knock your dick string loose 'n' send you in a nice little package to Hanoi with all the other hippy fucks! You can tell 'em jokes 'n' shit! You like that, boy? You like that?" The kid didn't know what to say, so he just stared straight ahead as the corporal kept screaming at him, spraying sweat and spit over his face.

Laying on the blacktop there, all tangled up together, is when we got our names. The three hats stopped yelling at us as we scrambled to our feet and ran to the line. The corporal, though, wasn't through. He moved to the fourth rank where we were standing at attention and continued his harangue. "You see that big sonofabitch over there, boy?" the corporal screamed, his face in my face. I could see my reflection in his sunglasses, scared and sweating, breathing heavy through my nose and waiting to get hit. It occurred to me I'd never been that close to a black man before. Hell, I'd never been that close to any man, and I really didn't like it. "You see him?" I nodded my head up and down and immediately knew it was the wrong move. "Don't you go noddin' your head at me, peckerhead! You say, 'Yes, Corporal,' as loud as you can when I talk to you. You got that, surga?"

"Yes, Corporal," I screamed, looking at myself in his sunglasses and waiting to get hit for sure.

"Well, that's Sergeant First Class Bobby Lee Boatright, 'n' he's the toughest drill sergeant in the United States Army. You see him?" The corporal waited, and I didn't know what to do. I couldn't see the man he was pointing at, and I was learning not to move my head. So I yelled "Yes, Corporal!" and let it go at that.

"He owns your ass. Bin to Vietnam two times, bin in Korea, bin in Panama, 'n' all over the Federal Republic of Germany. Bin shot three times, 'n' got the Silver Star for gallantry. Hates gooks almost as much as he hates little baby soldiers that can't even get off a bus without fuckin' up. Like you 'n' that lanky partner of yours. He hates it when your partner is late...Fucks his whole day up 'n' makes him angry. 'N' when he's angry, everyone suffers! You got that?"

"Yes, Corporal!" I was getting the hang of it now.

"So 'cause your partner there, Mr. Late, 'n' you, Mr. Too Late, couldn't unass the bus like soldiers, everybody gets down!" He looked at the file, and all the hats except for one started screaming, "Ged down! Ged down 'n' knock 'em out! Push-ups till Sergeant Boatright ain't angry no more! Ged down, maggots, 'n' push 'em out!" So there we were on the black tarmac, the oil and tar wet in the sun, burning our hands as we did five, then ten, then twenty push-ups and fell onto our bellies. It seemed, at that early stage of our training, twenty push-ups was our collective limit. Some made it to twenty-five, and O'Neal even did thirty, which he explained later as the residua of his high school football career in Newark. But most of us were out at twenty, laying flat and panting, gasping for air in the heat. Except for Danny. Next to me in the line, he kept going, slow and sure, up and down, smiling that grin and counting. "Twenty-five...thirty, thirty-one, thirty-two... forty." His movements were slow and deliberate and beautiful to watch, and if I hadn't been trying to gather any available oxygen into my lungs, and if I hadn't been so scared of what was going to come next, I would have rolled over on my back and clapped. But, of course, that wouldn't do.

"Ladies, I said knock 'em out! Get your bellies off the ground now! No wonder you pussies come in the army. Your girlfriends don't want you; peckerheads can't do no push-ups, no ups 'n' down for the girls back home. Ain't this some sorry shit!" The corporal turned away and spoke to the large hat who had his arms crossed. This must be Sergeant Boatright, I thought. "Sergeant Boatright, I'm sorry to say this is your new platoon! Looks to be the worst one we've seen yet. A sorry pack a draft dodgers 'n' national guard humps hidin' from Uncle Sam 'n' Charlie. But we're gonna make some kinda' soldiers out of 'em, if we have to kill every other one just to get the job done. We got platoon run in an hour. Can I send 'em into the barracks to secure their gear before we go play?" Boatwright nodded and, shaking his head back and forth, walked away toward the building we later learned was the mess hall. I looked over and Danny was still doing push-ups, slower now since nobody was watching, but still one every now and then to let the corporal know he wasn't done.

"OK, you peckerheads. We goin' in the barracks now. You got twenty minutes to find your rack, put your duffel bag in your locker, secure it with your new lock and key, and return to this exact location. Twenty goddamn minutes, army time. Not twenty-two minutes, not twenty-five minutes. Heh Late, stop the push-ups. You ain't impressin' no one!"

And Danny stopped and screamed, "Yes, Corporal!" as loud as he could. And we were gone.

In the barracks there were big rooms full of bunks, eight and ten to a room, and little rooms with only two bunks. Since nobody knew anybody else's name, we couldn't help each other as we searched the bunks for the name tags affixed to the steel springs. Everyone was running fast, room to room, screaming out names and moving on until he found his bunk. "Johnson, here! Geronimo! Johnson, here! Lewis! O'Neil! Kryzinski? What kinda name is that? Here's another Johnson! Joy! Oh boy, another damn Johnson!" All the names were flying through the air, and it was hard to determine where they were coming from. "Colt!" I heard it and started running down the hall toward the sound. As I turned the corner into a small room, I ran into Danny's duffel bag, which was on the floor. I fell right over it and landed at his feet. He was looking into his locker and ripping his new lock from the package.

"It appears we're roommates, Colt. My name's Joy, Danny Joy, from upstate New York. Welcome to the army." And that was when I first noticed that quality in his voice and actions that always seemed so comforting. He didn't appear to be more than twenty, maybe less, and had the tall, brushed looks of a guy who knew where he was and what he was about. There wasn't any panic in his eyes, and he didn't look scared. In fact, he looked like he belonged in that room, messing with his lock and getting ready for the next round with the hats. Indeed, he looked so normal he was out of place in the gaggle of scared, exhausted, sweating boys dragging their duffel bags up the stairs, around the corners and into the rooms. He was way ahead of the rest of us, and I made a mental note to stay close to him. In the survivor's logic, he seemed to know what he was doing and that might save me from some drastic painful mistake in the future. And besides, although I didn't know it at the time, he and I would spend every waking and sleeping hour together for eight weeks. And then, I thought in the shorthand I was getting used to, another eight weeks to learn infantry training and then maybe a year together in Vietnam. There were a lot of places on that journey to get in trouble, and I knew I really couldn't do it alone. Standing there scared and confused, looking for a way out of all this future misery and experiencing a small glimpse of what was to come, I knew I would need some help. "Knock my dick string loose"? What was that? Would Charlie really cut my dick off if I went to sleep? Had they imported some enemy prisoners to Fort Dix to harass us as part of the training? Who knew? It was that moment when I attached myself to this gangly kid from upstate New York and never let go.

We ran that day and every day thereafter, first in the morning as the sun was coming up and then later in the evening as the sun was going down. Sometimes we ran before lunch, and other times we ran after doing sit-ups and push-ups. Sometimes we ran with our heavy packs and sleeping bags; sometimes we ran with our rifles; always, we ran with our heavy leather boots and our fatigues dripping with sweat and often caked with dust or mud. We ran down the tarmac in front of the other basic training companies and then by the airfield and into the pine trees. Long runs in the sand. Six miles to the rifle ranges; three miles to the Advanced Infantry Barracks, the Old Third as we learned to call it; two miles to the clinic to get our shots; one mile to the PT field where we would take physical training tests and then run back. July at Fort Dix was a very hot place to run and so some got sick and fell out; others got sick and went to the hospital; others just fell down and were taken away, never to return. We ran until we weren't sore anymore, until the baby fat fell away. We ran until it was comfortable and we could talk, at least whisper, between ourselves as we ran. We ran until it stopped hurting and became natural. And sometimes, when we weren't being punished, we ran for fun.

Danny was in the squad next to me, and so we could whisper as we ran.

"You never been to the Hudson valley, have you?" Danny asked as we crossed the road near the airfield and adjusted our minds to the running in the sand. It was hot even though it was still dark, and we couldn't see much, other than the man in front of us. Danny ran straight up, his lungs wide open and efficient, processing the humid air and translating it into energy like the best kind of tuned engine. My gait was more stilted, bent over, and tortured. I ran with my mind, pushing my legs and arms and working hard, overworking on one cylinder. For that reason, I sucked more air and always let Danny do most of the talking. I grunted a no and set my eyes on Sergeant Boatright, running backward in the sand beside us.

"Let's go, ladies! Close it up there!" We were in our third week and getting used to the routine of it all. Boatright up front or on the side. Always watching, never really swearing, rarely saying more than was absolutely necessary. The corporal in the rear with a stick, hitting kids in the legs and pushing them back into ranks if they tried to fall out; he was always threatening, always cursing, endlessly in a state of apoplexy about our inability to accomplish the tasks he had set us to. Like a rabid dog. We were aware that Boatright might let him off his leash if we stepped out of line; although we were fairly sure the corporal wasn't authorized to kill anyone, there was some disagreement about how far Boatright would let him go. The corporal could hit you; spit on you; make you do push-ups; scare you into puking or pissing in your pants; and worse, he might recommend you to be recycled. Sent back to start over with another company; to endure the eight weeks over and over again for two years; never going to Vietnam but never leaving the tarmac and the hats, the noise, and the pain of it all. We mostly agreed that would be worse and so we ran and hauled and sang and jumped and tried not to ever fall out and wind up in the back with the corporal, alone and out of the pack. So far, with Danny's encouragement, I stayed right in the middle—next to Danny, right behind O'Neal, and in front of Geronimo. I learned to like that spot, not up front with the regular army guys who had volunteered for all this shit and not with the national guard and reserve guys who were volunteers of a kind, even if they were going home in six months. No, back with the other draftees, putting in our time and saying as little as possible. We were forming our own tribe as we lined up last for everything: last for chow, last for weapons inspection, last for letters and time to go to the PX. Danny was quietly becoming our leader.

"Well, you ain't seen nothin' till you seen the Hudson Valley at harvest time." Danny would start talking as we ran and keep on talking even as the rest of us were sucking wind and wondering if the run would ever stop. But after a while, Danny's stories got to be part of the run, and we all kind of looked forward to them. The miles would go by and, if you listened real hard, Danny could transform you out of that pine and sand and back to some place where the air was always cool and breezy. "First there's the sun to look at and then the river and mountains, all like a picture. You see? There's a whole lot of forest and just some small towns down next to the riverbank, some small bridges where other streams come into the big river and back roads, some of 'em paved and some of 'em dirt 'n' rock, which we use to move the harvest down to the trucks when it's harvest time. Our farm goes right down to the river. The rest is all orchards growin' apples and pears all over the sides of the hills. And I'm tellin' you, this time of year when the bees are buzzing 'round that fruit, the whole place smells like one big apple pie coming out of the oven."

O'Neal never liked the idea of all that forest, but he loved to listen to the stories nonetheless. He would turn his head slightly so Boatright wouldn't see him. "You got any bears in that forest?"

"Sure we do, little brown ones and then sometimes a big black one comes rangin' through," and then we would hear about camping trips up in the mountains past Albany when Danny was a kid. He and his father would wander out into the woods until there was no sign of human life and set up camp by a lake or stream and just fish. Fish and sleep for a week. They would sit and sleep, fish and sleep, swim and sleep, drink a beer and sleep. But mostly, according to Danny or at least according to what I remember, they would sleep in the cool air, nobody screaming at them and nothing much to do. Danny would talk about his family too, a brother named George, older by a couple of years, who had been in the army and served in Germany. George worked in Albany as a bus driver and went to college on the GI Bill at night. He didn't like camping much, so he rarely came back to their house. Danny would go to Albany to see him. And he would talk about his mom. He had a picture he would show us after lights out in the barracks when the corporal would finally stop walking the halls and go down to his office on the first floor. She was a pretty lady, blond and plump, working in the kitchen with an apron on. He said she was making apple pies and that when we got some leave we could go on up to upstate New York and she would make us a fine dinner with apple pie and pumpkin pie for dessert. He said that after the harvest in the fall, there were so many apples around that he would always have apple pie for breakfast too. Apple pie and a big glass of cold milk to go with it. He sure could get you going.

One night after the run, I think it was in our fifth or sixth week, the corporal walked through the barracks and stopped at our open door. "Late, get your gear. You 'n' Too Late here are goin' on guard mount up at battalion. You got one hour to get it together to stand the mount. Shine them boots 'n' wear your best fatigues. You make us look bad 'n' you guys won't be late…You'll be gone!" Ominous stuff, guard mount. We had heard about it from the other companies when we met them at the PX. Stand real straight with a bunch of guys from the rest of the companies, get inspected, and answer any questions the officer might ask. No fooling around and no mistakes. Then go out in the dark and guard the mess hall or the PX or the golf course all night. But the best two—those guys got to guard the general's office at headquarters, and stay inside and sleep. Sometimes there would be coffee and cake left over by the secretaries, and if not, at least you could rack out for a while without the corporal jumping in your shit all night.

"We can do this," Danny announced and gathered up his brush and polish. Down to the latrine we strolled, while the rest of the platoon left for the mess hall. We set up quick in the shower area where we could do our boots without getting polish on the floor around our bunks. Danny had this down, and I followed his moves like his was the only way to shine boots. Because like everything else in the army, there was a trick to this. It was a trick that some knew and others didn't. Those that knew prospered, and those that didn't suffered until they found out, got the information, and mastered the task. It was the same drill whether it was firing your weapon, cleaning your gas mask, or shining your boots. Find out the trick, practice the task, and master the task. Some guys had it, and the rest of us watched and waited for the pain. But that night, Danny took me through the ritual so we could both get to sleep in the general's office. "Late and Too Late…sleepin' late," we said, giggling, and commenced to get it done.

Each of us had two pairs of boots, and the smart guys ignored the sergeant's instructions to switch off each day. Instead, they kept one set of boots for the woods and the other for wearing around the blacktop where we mostly got inspected and punished for looking like shit. My boots were all tore up from wearing them in the woods and on the ranges while Danny's second set were like new. "We're gonna have to do some real work on that set of boonie boots there," Danny exclaimed. "Here, you start on my set, just get the dust off them, and apply a layer of polish. I'll start working on yours." First, we washed them in the sink, getting all the dust and crap out from in between the creases and the soles. Then Danny took his can of black shoe polish and placed it on a bench. He took a lighter from his pocket and lit the polish on fire. It burned with a black smoke and went liquid almost immediately. Then, he took the tip of his shoe rag, dipped it, and applied it around the lip of the boots and then all over the front and sides. He worked on the tongue too and made sure there was no part of those boots that hadn't been doused. Each scratch was filled in, each gouge disappeared. He looked over at me and smiled. "You goin' to be the prettiest soldier at the ball tonight, Private Too Late." He motioned at the boot I was holding. "Now you get started. We've only got another forty-five minutes to go, forty-five army minutes, peckerhead!" He mocked the corporal, and we both laughed. We rubbed the boots down and brushed the sides and the tips until they shined all black and clean. Danny took the other side of the rag, wrapped it tightly around his trigger finger, and dipped into a cup he had filled with water from the tap. He started to apply the water in a circular motion to the tip of the boot, round and round until the shine changed. He would take just a touch of polish and apply it to the tip, rub it in, and then go back to his circular motion with the water, all the time making sure the water was clean. "See that?" he looked up with the eye of a criminal co-conspirator. "That's what makes 'em shine. Makes a spit shine and a ticket to the general's office! Now you do it." And of course I really didn't have time to get the hang of it—making the tip of a shoe or boot shine like a piece of black glass—and to this day I still can't make a shoe look like Danny could.

But I gave it a pretty good try, and when it came to the touch-up and the final touches on all four boots, Danny finished them off. We ran back to our bunks, dressed like we were going to a dinner party, and went to the supply room to draw our weapons.

"Where you young studs all dressed up goin' to?" That drawl was unmistakable, and we both froze as we stood in front of the rifle cage waiting for the supply clerk to issue us our rifles. Sergeant Boatright walked over from the shadows on the other side of the supply room where he was apparently reading the newspaper and drinking coffee. "I'm not goin' ta ask you twice," he said quiet-like as he approached us. We turned around and stood at attention. He walked up to me and got into my face, looked my uniform up and down, and stared at my boots in astonishment. "Where'd you learn to shine boots like that, Colt? You ain't some kinda ringer from a military academy or somethin' are you?" I felt like I had been found out; my secret was public, and I was going straight to hell. But I didn't know what the secret was, and I couldn't think of how to answer Sergeant Boatright.

"No Sergeant, he ain't no ringer," Danny answered. "I showed him the trick. You know, using wet polish and spit shining the tips. We're goin' to guard mount, and we didn't want to embarrass the platoon." There was some serious quiet for a minute or two during which Sergeant Boatright considered this information. He wanted to ask Danny if he was a ringer, I know he did, but he didn't do it. Instead, he turned around and walked back to his coffee. "Well, don't be late. Check each other's gig lines just before you fall in. Platoon's countin' on you," he said over his shoulder.

We got our equipment and got out of there before Sergeant Boatright thought of anything else to say. One thing you learn in the army, especially if you're a draftee and looking to just do your time and get back out on the street: you don't hang around officers or anybody else in authority more than is absolutely necessary. They generally don't want you around, and you can only wind up in some kind of trouble, piss somebody off for no reason, or do something wrong. Even forty years later, I'm not much for standing in lines or getting in people's faces. It just isn't in me to stand up in front unless I have to. As we left, though, me with my head down and my eyes on the back door of the bay, Danny looked back and smiled at Sergeant Boatright there in the shadows. "Don't worry, Sergeant, we won't let you down." And we were gone.

In formation at battalion headquarters, we had 'em all beat by a mile right from the beginning. First a drill came out, called us to attention, and inspected all twenty of us soldiers from different companies, one at a time. He was in our face checking to make sure we shaved; he checked our weapons to see if they were clean and properly oiled, and he looked down at our boots. Fortunately, Danny and I had checked each other out before we got in the line, so our buttons lined up with our belt buckles and the flies of our trousers. Danny got no gigs, and I only received one deficiency for some hair on the back of my neck. The rest of the men didn't have that kind of luck. When the sergeant major came out, the drill called us back to attention, and we waited for him to go over us once again. I think the drill had spoken to the sergeant major inside though, because when he got to Danny and me, he really didn't inspect us all that closely. "You Boatright's people?" the sergeant major growled. He was tall like Boatright but heavier, and he was black as Danny's boots. He had short gray hair clipped on the sides so tight it looked shined, and his uniform was starched almost white.

"Yes, Sergeant Major!" we both yelled. It was about five thirty, and we could hear a bugle begin to play as the flag was being taken down from the post flagpole somewhere behind the building. The sergeant major did an about-face as smart as any I've ever seen and yelled "Detail, Preesent Harms!" We all saluted with our rifles and waited until the bugle stopped. And then we waited a minute or so after that in silence, the wind cracking in our ears and, off in the distance, a plane coming from some unknown destination, landing on the airfield across the road. "Horder...Harms!" The sergeant major pronounced. He turned around and looked straight at Danny. "Tell Sergeant Boatright he's doin' a pretty good job down there." He walked back into the headquarters building and we got to stand at ease.

Well, of course, that was the tip-off that we had won the day. Danny got the number one spot—the super numerary or something, and I was his backup. We got our choice of what we wanted to do, and Danny told them we wanted to guard the general's office. The drill put us in the back of a truck, and off we went. He let us off in the front of the building with instructions to go to the second floor and see the sergeant, who would tell us what to do. The drill said he would be back to pick us up for reveille the next morning, and we better be ready. No sleeping on duty and all that. He made Danny the senior soldier of our two-man detail and drove away to post the rest of the troops around. Cake and coffee and rack time was what we were thinking as we climbed the stairs.

The sergeant let us in and gave us the instructions. They were typed on a piece of paper backed with cardboard and laminated. At the top of the board there was a chain, and the sergeant hung the board around my neck. "Now you listen up, and you listen up good. This here's the general's office, his secretary's office, the conference room, the kitchen, and the aid's office. You don't leave these offices except once an hour when you go around the whole building checking the outside doors, the windows, and the fire escapes. I don't want no vandalism, no fires, no messin' 'round with the stuff on the desks, and especially no grab ass. You hear?" And then he read us each word of the instructions, which pretty much said where to go during the night and what not to touch. He picked up a large coffee thermos and let himself out without any more talk. Guess he wasn't a drill sergeant, because he didn't seem to have a desire to bust our chops. He just went home or wherever else sergeants go when their day is done. It was seven thirty and the building was quiet.

We immediately checked out the kitchen and found a box full of cookies and a note from one of the secretaries: "You boys can eat the cookies and make one pot of coffee, but don't touch anything else. In the morning before you leave, make a fresh pot of coffee. The general likes his coffee when he comes in at six o'clock." Danny grabbed a cookie and went and sat on the couch in the secretary's office. "Well, this is surely some kinda' fine," he exclaimed. I kept looking over my shoulder half-expecting the sergeant or the general to come strolling in, but Danny seemed thoroughly relaxed. And so the night went. By midnight we had checked the building five times, wandering through the hallways with our flashlights and tugging on each lock to make sure there were no security violations. Each time we would return to the kitchen, grab a cookie and some coffee, and go into the conference room. About two, we changed our routine and got up enough nerve to go into the general's office. It was large and neat as a pin. There wasn't any garbage in the garbage can, and there weren't any papers on the desk. The chair was big and brown, covered in leather, and the back of the wall was draped with a two-star general's flag and a stars-and-stripes flag. On the desk there were a chrome bayonet and an ashtray made out of a brass artillery shell, with an inscription that read, "Captain Rodney B. Davis, Korea 1952." On the wall there were pictures, lots of them. They mostly showed the general in Korea and Vietnam in fatigues, unshaven with a helmet and a rifle, surrounded by other guys looking dirty and unshaven. Each had a date and the name of a unit, and a lot of them were faded and cracked.

"Looks like the general's been around," Danny whispered. The thoughts of war, those thoughts that always hung just below the surface of any conversation, were thick that evening. Guys would wonder about it all. Were the hats really telling us the truth about Charlie, about fighting in the dark, about not being able to sleep for a year, about all that killing and body bags and taking-care-of-your-buddy stuff? When we sang, "I wanna go to Vietnam, I wanna kill some Viet Cong," what did we mean? Each wondered quietly in the morning, in his sleep, in the moments in the dark as taps played through the air, whether he would measure up, remember all the things we were learning, and not fuck up and kill somebody. There was the possibility of blowing up a buddy; shooting some poor, dumb gook civilian kid; or eating a grenade. It seemed like there were so many ways to kill and be killed. You clearly had to pay attention. But if you couldn't sleep, how could you remember everything and react fast enough to take care of yourself and the rest of the guys who were depending on you? If you couldn't even spit shine a boot, how could you master all the other tasks, get the right information, and do the right thing?

"I think I'm gonna have problems when we get over there," I said, surprising myself for saying out loud what I was thinking. Danny was eating a cookie and sitting in the general's big chair. Somehow, he looked like he belonged there. He stood up, put his hands on his hips, squared away his shoulders and strutted around to the front of the desk. He stared down at me and started in.

"I'll tell you somethin', Mista Too Late," Danny said, sliding into the corporal's jargon. "You just stay close to whatever sergeant is sorry enough to get you in his platoon. Do whatever that sombitch tells you, 'n' you gonna be all right. 'Cause they got a whole new set of rules over dere, ya see? Simple rules like don't bunch up, 'n' clean your weapon, 'n' drink enough water, 'n' watch out for the guy next to ya, 'n' stay awake when you're supposed to, 'n' sleep when ya can. If yer on point, you watch out for booby traps 'n' ambushes 'n' such. If not, you watchin' out to the sides of the trail. If you in the back, you lookin' behind you. Write your momma, keep your feet clean, and count the days. All this other shit's just practice ta get you to listen when the important stuff comes along. Soon enough, you be back in the world, pickin' apples with Mr. Late there 'n' happier 'n' a pig in shit." Now those were rules I could understand, and as I settled back in the chair and drank my coffee, I relaxed for the first time in weeks. How he knew that, how he'd figured it all out, I don't know. He seemed to like the army life, or at least he was good at it. His advice cleared a lot of things up for me and made the rest of the training pretty easy.

We graduated on a fine warm day in the middle of September. The night before, the corporal came around the barracks and showed us how to starch and iron our khaki uniforms. He was a lot friendlier than he had been, and even when he called us "peckerheads" he didn't yell at us when we laughed at him. We shined our belt buckles so the lacquer was all wiped off, and our shoes were spit shined to a perfect sheen. We packed all our crap neatly into our duffle bags and dragged them down to the tarmac. And then we got into formation and marched. Most of us, especially the draftees in the back, were going across the base to the Old Third, out in the woods, to begin Advanced Infantry Training. A lot of the guys who'd signed up, the RAs, had big envelops with orders and their personnel records stuffed into their new black overnight bags and were heading to the bus station for other posts, where they would learn to be cooks or intelligence guys or something else—anything else but infantrymen. And the National Guard guys were grab-assing, because they knew that in just four more months they'd be home again. They never took any of this seriously, and we both envied them and hated them for their carelessness. They would forget all this soon enough, and go back to school like it never happened and didn't mean anything. They were beating the system, and they never missed a chance to let us know how much smarter they were then us. But we also thought they were somehow less than real soldiers, still boys staying close to home and their mommas. They had our envy for sure but not our respect.

Danny was standing in front of the formation. He had been chosen the platoon guide, a sort of temporary sergeant, picked by the hats to organize the rest of us when the corporal and the sergeants weren't around. As a company of new recruits came by, we watched them trying to march, looking scared, all fat and sweating. They didn't know how to march in step, couldn't wear their uniforms properly, and carried their packs like so much garbage. Not squared away. Danny yelled, "Attenshun!" and we all snapped to. "About-face!" he ordered, and we turned on our heels and toes, keeping our arms straight down the seams of our pants, not flailing around. "Present arms!" We saluted those poor bastards and smiled, content in the knowledge that we had a secret they didn't know and couldn't discover without weeks and weeks of training. Frankly, it felt wonderful, and we were happy that Danny had thought to show us off.

Then the hats came out of the mess hall. Each was dressed in his green uniform with badges and ribbons earned through long careers. It was the first time we had seen them all dressed up, shoes spit shined, creases sharp as knives, combat infantryman's badges and parachute wings gleaming. And ribbons. By now we could read the ribbons—the Silver Star on Boatright's chest, the Purple Hearts, the Air Medals. Bronze Stars with "V" devices for valor. Each sergeant wore his resume on his chest, and we were proud that they were our leaders. Boatright marched to the front of the formation, and Danny saluted him. "The platoon is formed, Sergeant," Danny said, loud enough for all of us to hear him.

"Take your post," Boatright growled, and he returned the salute so efficiently that we were all startled. It was perfect—his fingers together, tilted slightly forward, just barely touching the tip of his hat; his shoulders back, his left hand curled and resting on the seam of his trousers. He moved the hand up slowly but brought it down crisply. It was a display, but it was also a demonstration that he knew what he was doing and had mastered all the skills necessary to be a soldier. Danny did an about-face and moved to the side of the formation. "You men have completed your training here. We gonna be happy to send you out into the army to learn more skills, so's you can go to war and beat the snot out of the enemy. You soldiers now, 'n' I look forward to seeing some of you in the Nam. I'll be happy to serve with you there. Go learn what you need to, and I'll see you again on the trail." He called for the corporal, who came to the front of the formation. "Take these men to Doughboy field and graduate them, Corporal. We got work to do!"

And so we marched to the field, lined up with other companies who were graduating, and spent an hour listening to some colonel talk about how strong we were and how the nation needed us. There were some parents there, but mostly it was just some old guys sitting in the bleachers, wearing VFW hats and American flag pins on their lapels. The audience didn't matter. We stood on that mowed grass together among those with whom we had spent all those hours separated from everything we had known—our civilian friends and families; the politics of the war; and the girls who had stopped writing us, who we had left behind. And really, graduation had already occurred when Boatright saluted us and wished us well. Boatright never said much, but what he said mattered, and we were proud to stand in the sun of that fine warm day and receive his blessing for the first and last time.

Advanced Infantry Training (AIT) was both a lot easier and a lot harder. For one thing, there were a new set of rules to follow, and that confused us. Gone were the screaming hats, attached to us like leaches, organizing our every waking and sleeping hour: "You goin' to sleep now, boy, 'cause in five hours I'm gonna be right here ready to run your sorry ass off, down the trail and into the woods. Army says you allowed sleepin' some, 'n' now's the time. Ready…Sleep!" There were still hats, but they were more like caretakers; getting us up, making sure we had the right equipment to go to the field, and marching us off into the woods to meet with other sergeants. Those sergeants trained us in everything from claymore mines, to booby traps, to M60 machine guns, to how to spot an ambush on the trail. On Friday nights we would come back to the barracks and spend the night cleaning it up so we could get inspected by some officer on Saturday morning, who would appear out of nowhere and then leave. Demerits listed and punishments awarded. And then, if we didn't have to go on funeral detail and didn't have too many demerits, we were off until Sunday night at 1900 hours. We could leave Fort Dix and go home; spend the weekend in the battalion beer joint, the slop shute or maybe go to the movies or just hang around and sleep.

At first, we all stayed in the barracks. We didn't have much money, and we weren't sure if they would really let us off the base if we tried to leave. O'Neil, we thought, had it about right: "If you try to leave, they know it. See, you got your greens on and you look like a trainee, so's they knows you right away. 'N' if you come back late, you awol. Absent without fucking leave. That's when they really got you. They give you an Article 15 or court-martial your ass—send you back to another company to start training all over again. Better just to hang out. I'm tellin' you man, you can't trust 'em."

But Danny left the first weekend they let us out. He said he had to get home and help out with the harvest. Apples were getting picked, and if you didn't take them down when they were ripe, you lost the whole season. They would rot there on the trees, or the birds would get them. Then the frost would come, and it would be all over. He put on his greens, stuffed a pair of jeans and a sweat shirt into his overnight bag; and headed out the gate, hitchhiking all the way to the Hudson valley. When he got back at 1630, a half hour before the formation that checked to see if we were all present for duty, he seemed changed. Agitated and distant. Unlike the rest of us, he had been out in the world, and it had changed him. "So how was it?" I asked him as we were heading back to the slop shute for more beer after the formation. "You see any girls?"

The slop chute was a Korean War barracks like the one we slept in on the weekends. Our home was a platoon-sized, clapboard structure, painted white, with a coal heater at one end and windows painted shut throughout. Hot in the afternoon, cold in the morning, and crammed full of bunk beds and footlockers. It was pretty broken down, but after all our work, we knew it was clean. Of course, in the slop chute there were no bunks. In the corner was a jukebox, and at the other end was a wooden bar with taps of 3.2 beer and pitchers lined up on a shelf. The walls were painted with different company mottos and pictures of infantrymen slogging through the jungle of Vietnam. Trainees had scribbled on the walls, and the floors were filthy, with spilled beer and cigarette butts everywhere. It was a shit-hole for sure, but at least there were no sergeants around, and for two dollars a guy could get fairly shit-faced without anyone caring.

"Nah," Danny answered, looking down as we walked the path to get a beer. The path was gravel and trimmed with white painted rocks that we touched up on Friday evenings as part of our inspection routines. There was a sign in front of the building that read "Slopchute" and scribbled underneath it the statement "Ave, Imperator, morituri te salutant, We who are about to die, salute you." GI humor at its best. "No time. I spent the rest of Saturday and this morning in the orchards getting the apples down. My dad gave me some money to get a bus back, but he's screwed. For some reason, there's no apple pickers this year. Or at least not enough." He thought for a while. "I don't know what he's gonna do."

They had us in full combat gear for the six-mile hike to the field the next day. We had our sleeping bags, packs; extra socks and razors, gas masks, entrenching tools, shelter halves, pegs and lines; M14s with bayonets, of course; and all the other crap that hung on our web gear. Our steel helmets bounced on our heads, and our pockets were filled with candy and cans of food from the PX. Food in the field came in steel containers twice a day from the back of a truck. It was often cold, and there was never enough of it. We were getting used to improvising. Long marches hurt but were how infantrymen got around. And we always had someplace to go, and we were always late.

"So's you see any girls?" O'Neil asked as we trudged along the trail. "Got to get outta here 'n' see some girls. Man, I'm about to blow up iffen I don't get me a girl soon." O'Neil was the one guy who had a girl come to visit him during basic training, a tall black chick with great legs and a shiny afro haircut. She wore tall heels and a miniskirt. Over the weeks, my dreams of girls I had known had faded like so many memories, replaced by O'Neil's girl. She, at least, showed up when you needed her.

"No time," Danny grunted. "Too much to do."

"Now that's where you got it all wrong, Late. There's never too much to do when it comes to girls." He broke into a song by Otis Redding. "'You got to hold her, never squeeze her, never leave her, now get to her, and try a little tenderness.'" I chuckled and looked over at O'Neil who, being black, was the acknowledged stud in the platoon, at least acknowledged by us white guys.

"Yeah, well, maybe next time," Danny muttered. Something was wrong though. Danny wasn't laughing. He was bent over and far away; not talking about orchards and the smell of apples; not going on and on about how fall was the time to pick them and clean them, cook them and eat them. When we hit the range and sat in the bleachers listening to some sergeant go on about cover and concealment, he didn't volunteer to be the test case when the instructor asked for one. Danny always volunteered. Later, after chow and cleaning the tents, we were sitting under the pines as the sun went down, smoking and drinking the last of the hot coffee we had made. That was always the best time of the day. It wasn't hot anymore but not cold yet either. The sun would go down, and the muscles could loosen up there under the trees. Crickets and birds would be chirping. That's when you finally had time to stop and take it all in.

"What you thinkin' about for next weekend?" I asked him. I was getting up the nerve to take my own trip home and wondered if he wanted to come with me. I'd never hitchhiked before and was looking for some company. Besides, we all kind of knew that time was running out. A few more weeks and then we would be done, receive orders, and off to Vietnam.

"I gotta get back home," he sighed. "There's a shit-load more apples to harvest and nobody else to do it. Besides," he almost whispered, "I kinda miss the place." He field-stripped his cigarette, put the filter in his pocket, and lit another one. "You ever think about going home?" he asked me.

"Sure, that's what I'm gonna do this weekend. I want you to come with me. I think I can get us a couple of dates, or at least we can sit around my house and watch some TV. Who knows? God knows the food will be better."

Danny thought for a while, looked up at the top of a pine, and watched some squirrels run from branch to branch. "Yeah, well, that ain't gonna happen. Sorry 'bout that." He was resigned to something, and I knew not to push it.

"OK, maybe next time," I said, my voice trailing off as the sun went down, and we headed back to the tents to sleep.

I did make it home that weekend; I hitchhiked up the turnpike in my greens and some nice guy took me out of his way, into my hometown, and right to my house. "Was in Korea, kid," he said as he let me off. "Now you watch out over there, take it slow, and come on back to us." I nodded and thanked him. It was the first acknowledgement by somebody other than a soldier that I was really going to war, and it startled me. This wasn't all training and bullshit. We were on a trail that ended in a very bad place, and there didn't seem to be a way to get off. At least me and Danny would run the trail together, though—Late and Too Late jumping through hoops until it was all over and done with.

What happened at home that weekend wasn't really much to tell about. And anyway, it's the subject of another story. Danny wasn't there; he'd gone back to the Hudson Valley and his apples. Suffice it to say, I didn't get even close to getting laid. I took the bus back and made it by 1900 hours, although it was close.

Danny wasn't in formation at 1900 hours, and that scared the hell out me. He was, however, at the slop chute, seriously drunk and seriously pissed off. "Heh, the first sergeant's looking for you, man," I said, as I sat down and poured a beer into a plastic cup from the pitcher in front of Danny. He was sitting alone at a table in the corner of the chute, staring at the wall. The place was all noisy and full of smoke. Two guys from another company were chugging beers, as a bunch of other guys consulted their watches to see who finished first. One cup crashed down on the table next to us and fell to the floor. The guy burped long and hard and sat down. Everyone else was yelling and paying off bets. "That's two dollas you owe me," the winner said, and he poured himself another cup.

"Fuck the first sergeant," Danny mumbled. "I ain't goin' to see him and I ain't going back to the barracks. I'm just gonna sit here 'n' finish this pitcher." He poured himself another beer. "And then I'm goin' home."

I was shocked; I mean, I was bowled over. "What, are you crazy?" I all but screamed. "We only got two more weeks in this shit-hole and then we're outta here. Two weeks leave and then we're gone. You can't just up and leave!" The idea of going home early, telling the army to go fuck itself, had simply never occurred to me. Each week there were guys who did it, didn't show up at Sunday formation and were dropped from the rolls, never to be heard from again. Disappeared. One time we thought we saw one of them, a guy we knew from basic called "Swingin' Johnson," mostly because of the size of his dick and the fact that there were three other Johnsons in the company. He was trudging along at the back of a brand new AIT company, keeping to himself, going through the training over again. It was incomprehensible to us how a guy could do this crap one more time. "Shit," O'Neil had said, "there's no way. I mean no fucking way I do this again. Iffen I break 'n' go awol, I'm just gonna keep on goin'. Head to Africa or Argentina or some damn place. Somewhere they can't find me. 'Cause I ain't never gonna line up in formation with rookies again. Without you guys, this shit simply ain't doable again. That damn trail's seen enough a me!" Most of us felt the same way. It was just too hard a thing to contemplate. And here was Danny, of all people, getting ready to take the plunge.

"What's going on?" I asked. "Somebody die?"

"Nah, everybody's fine." Danny finished his beer, lit a cigarette, and emptied the pitcher. "We need another here," he said, looking around. I got up and went to the bar, retrieved another pitcher, and sat down again. "But my dad's in a real trick bag. He's only got two more weeks to get all them apples in, or his season is lost. Apples rot, and he's got no money to make it through the rest of the year. He'll lose the farm and everything else. Christ!" He thought for a while. "I bin telling you guys how it works. The season is the season, and that's just the way it is. You don't fuck around with that..." he said, trailing off.

I was thinking as fast as I could, but nothing much was coming to mind. I mean, how do you beat the logic of nature? "Well, maybe if you go talk to the company commander, he'll understand and give you some time off to take care of business."

"Been there, done that," Danny said. "Talked to the first sergeant this afternoon—even brought him a letter from my dad. Told him I'd be glad to come back in three or four days, maybe a week; just enough time to get them over the hump. Finish up training and go on over to Vietnam with the rest of you guys. They could take the time off my leave. But the First Shirt says there's nothing he can do, no exceptions to the rule. Got to finish training on time like everybody else. Clearly," he mumbled, "that sombitch don't understand the apple-picking business."

O'Neil came into the chute and sat down next to us. "Bin lookin' for you guys," he muttered, as he filled a paper cup with beer from the pitcher. "Where you bin, Late?"

"Don't ask," I said.

"Man, it ain't right. I'm here. I'm shinin' my shoes, working at bein' the best soldier I can be, like my dad told me. All's I need is one damn favor and then I'm back. Go fight their war for them. Keep America safe 'n' all that shit. What they say, O'Neil? Army ain't got no soul? Nope, no soul indeed," he concluded. "Well, fuck 'em. I'm outta here."

O'Neil looked at me and shook his head. "You right, Late, o' course. But that don't mean you kin run off. They'll jus catch you 'n' send you back to the beginnin'. No," he said, "you can't run off."

"Sure, I can," Danny argued. "And I'm gonna." He put his cup down on the table and said, "Get me some more beer." O'Neil and I went up to the bar for another pitcher.

"We gotta help the boy out," O'Neil said, as we waited to be served. "He'll see it different in the mornin'. We just got to get him back to the barracks and tuck his skinny white ass in 'n' watch him. Watch 'em good until he sobers up. Ain't no way we let him outta here. That's just too fucked up."

When we went back to the table, Danny was all but passed out. O'Neil told him that if he wanted to go, he was going to need some sleep so it was better if we went back to the barracks and he got some shut-eye before he took off. Danny kind of agreed to that, and we all but carried him back to his bunk, laid him up in there, and considered our options. "Look, Too Late, you sit up with him for a couple of hours and then wake me up and I'll spell ya. That way we get through the night and then we'll talk his ass down in the mornin' 'fore chow." He thought some more. "Gimme his civilian clothes. He can't go nowhere without them. Hitchhikin' on a Monday in greens will get him caught for sure." And that's what we did. I sat on Danny's footlocker and smoked some, watching the fire guard walk through the barracks every so often to make sure nobody burnt the place down. "Fuckin' apples!" I thought.

In the morning, Danny woke up all hungover and sore. I felt the same way as I spied O'Neil sitting on the edge of Danny's bunk with a can of Coke and some crackers. "Let's get some chow, now. We gotta get ready to head to the field. You with us, Late?" Danny kind of smiled at us.

"Guess I put on a real bender last night. You guys get me back here?" And he seemed OK. In a way it felt like the storm had passed, so we really didn't think it was a good idea to mention it. "Gimme my clothes back. I got to put 'em in my locker before we head out." I looked at O'Neil and he nodded, went to his locker, and returned Danny's jeans and sweat shirt. "I'm going to take a long hot shower and get my shit together," Danny said. "You guys go on to chow, and bring me back a plate of eggs and some coffee." Danny was in charge again, and we followed his orders like always.

But when we got back, he was gone. His bedroll was all packed up, and his locker was empty except for his military gear. He'd skied, and there was nothing we could do about it. "Damn," O'Neil said. "I'm gonna miss that sombitch for sure."

Marching to the ranges the next two weeks was hard. Nobody to talk to and no stories from Danny, just a big hole next to me where he had always been. O'Neil and I partnered up a lot more, but it wasn't the same and we knew it. Even as things got easier there at the end, everything seemed harder. We were just trudging through; the rain got colder, the coffee weaker, and the sand seemed to weigh more as it stuck to our boots on the way to the field. O'Neil got in a fight with a small white sergeant about something and almost hit him. He was restricted to Dix for the rest of the cycle, and I stayed on base with him to keep him company. We were just pissed off all the time and nothing, not even graduation, helped.

We did graduate at the end of October, and most of us got our orders for Vietnam. Two weeks leave and then back to Dix to get on a plane. It was scary, of course, but neither O'Neil nor I could get up the energy to care. "Don't mean nothin'," O'Neil would mutter, "don't mean a goddamn thing." There was the same parade field, the same old guys in the bleachers and a different colonel talking about how important we all were to the country. They gave us infantry blue brassards and blue backings for our infantry brass to put on our greens. We shined up everything before we marched, but it didn't make much difference. We were on the trail and heading out no matter what we did. We didn't trust anybody anymore, so's none of it was fun.

And after that, we couldn't find a cab, so O'Neil and I had to drag our duffel bags to the bus station across base. As we left the company area, a group of trainees, just starting all that shit, marched by, heading to the field. In the back we saw Danny, bent over and sweating the trail. He looked like a convict, and he might as well have had shackles on his ankles. We wanted to stop and talk to him, but the company kept on moving, and there was no way he was going to break formation. Besides, we were embarrassed for him. Through all the weeks of that summer and fall, the one thing that kept us going, the one challenge was the constant taunt from the hats. "You ain't gonna make it, you peckerhead! You can't do this. You gonna run like the little pussy civilian you is!" And Danny had run, and for whatever reason, hadn't made it. He was alone and struggling. And so were we. We knew we were going to have to do the rest of this trail without him, and it damn near broke our hearts.

A SORTA WAR STORY

A guy once told me that war stories don't have to be true. Well, not completely true. They're always told after the fact, sometimes long after the fact, and generally in bars, or at least in places where people have loosened up. War stories are kinda like car wrecks; somethin' for sure happened, but who can remember the details? Especially if you were there and trying to keep your own ass from being blown away. They gotta smell right though. There can't be too much me in them. Mostly, they've got to be about other guys, or places and times. And they've got to feel right. Kinda like a good dream that wakes you up wondering where you are and if what you dreamed really happened. If you been in a real shoot-'em-up, you have a hard time figuring out what's true anymore, anyway. Guys who've been through that sort of thing understand that and don't much worry about the details anyhow.

I know this car wreck happened though, because I was there, and I hadn't blown dope for about a week and hadn't had a beer in five or six days. Sure, I was tired enough. We hadn't slept under a roof in a week, and it had been raining a lot as we sat in hedgerows on ambush each night. There's a kind of dreamy thing that happens to you when you're in that condition. You turn off all the bullshit around you—the colors, the weather, the endless discussions occurring between your buddies about girls and cars and shitty officers—but you tune into things that matter, like smells and short sparks of light and especially sounds of little people moving through the bush. You keep the sound of the guy next to you as he breathes in the dark real clear, and if it changes, it brings you back. I never much cared about bugs buzzing around my ears, but I sure as hell paid attention to rocks turning over and the metallic click of weapons.

That night, I'm in a team of six guys and two white mice, doing ambushes in this little town just south of Lai Khe in Vietnam, the Republic of. We're part of a recon platoon, and the rest of the guys get the night off. The lieutenant's in charge, and there's Poole, Dreamy, Shakes, Thompson, and me, with the two Vietnamese cops who normally wear white hats, which of course is why we call 'em white mice. The lieutenant's a couple of years older than the rest of us, been to OCS, and spent some time in the bush with a regular platoon. We could call him "sir" like they taught us in basic, but he settles for "LT" and that works for us. He's OK and generally does the right thing, especially when Poole and Dreamy are around to keep him straight. If there's something we don't like, Poole takes him off to the side and tells him. Most often he sees what we're talking about and changes the order or the plan or whatever. He covers for us with battalion too, so's we don't get put out there in the woods without support. And he makes sure we can get into Lai Khe every now and then to get laid, get drunk, and get some sleep. The LT's looking to get home in one piece himself and say good-bye to the green machine, so's he's not wasting time on the Mickey Mouse. As a rule, we do what he tells us, and all things considered, we're pretty happy with him. Believe me, we could have done a lot worse.

Anyway, that afternoon, Poole goes with the LT to have lunch with the mayor of the town. The rest of us lounge around the square, talking to the mamasans and giving candy to the kids. Dreamy is doing an unofficial MEDCAP with the locals, because he's a medic and has the pills and bandages to take care of the little shit that they come up with. The folks like the visits from the medics, so everything's copacetic. Poole brings a bottle of Jim Beam with him, and he and the LT sit around eating gook food and drinking bourbon. They try to get some intel out of the mayor as they talk, but it's hard. The mayor knows we're only going to be around for a few days, and he's going to have to deal with the VC when we're gone. On the other hand, the VC tax the shit out of the town and treat the people bad. They make some of the young studs go into the bush with them to fight for the cause, and sometimes they're not real nice to the girls either. The VC get real pissed when the civilians help us out though. Besides, the interpreter doesn't speak much English and gets pretty drunk after his first jar of bourbon.

The mayor and his people start to relax after the first round, and they make fun of the LT and Poole as they eat the gook food. First there's real hot pepper soup, mostly water and maybe a piece of chicken with hot pepper. Then there's this strange meat wrapped in transparent sheets of rice paper with all kinds of green vegetables and onions. The meat could be pig, chicken, rat, or some kind of lizard. It's hard to know because it's all boiled. If you're not careful, the LT says, you gonna gag on it for sure. Got to keep thinking chicken and not insult the mayor in front of his people.

At the end of the visit, the mayor is drunk and heads off to take a nap. The police chief is an old guy who looks like he's been survivin' the war for a lot of years. He's probably got some agenda of his own, but he takes the LT off to the side. "You caca dau VC?" he asks.

"Sure, we kill VC," the LT answers. "But we need to know what direction they're comin' in from." The chief looks around to see if anyone else is listening.

"Tonight, maybe five or ten come into north side. Get some boom boom and food. You ready?"

"You sure? Mebbe more, mebbe not so many? What you think?" The LT is, of course, leery. Too many gooks and there's a problem, since there's only six of us. We never count the white mice. We don't know 'em, they're not infantrymen anyway, and they could be VC themselves for all we know. We do know they must have fucked up pretty bad for their boss to send 'em out with us. We're sure they have what we call a morale problem, in any case. Hell, at the first sign of trouble, they're liable to strip down to their skivvies and melt into the bush. You just can never tell.

"Allays come in team five, ten. No coming for a week or so. Coming tonight for sure." The LT says thanks and hands the chief a carton of camels.

"You smoke 'em and relax. We caca dau bad guys for you. Sleep tight, Chief." The LT and Poole didi back to the square and gather us up.

Thompson comes riding into the square in one of our jeeps. He's all smiles and excitement. "Heh, Poole," he yells, "I got 'em!" He was sent back to the rear to get us some C rations and ammo. The LT is off in the corner of the square talking to battalion on the horn. We assume he's reporting on the intel and getting permission to set an ambush. Thompson's got four weapons in leather cases in the back of the jeep. Poole comes over and pulls them out. "Nice," he says, as he runs his hands over one of them. "Remington, 12-gauge, pump-action, semiautomatic shotgun. Carries eight rounds and kicks the shit out of anything within fifty feet." He pulls the handle back and plays with the safety. "Now this is a weapon!" Poole's from West Virginia and likes to think he's a cowboy. He carries a Colt .45 single-action army revolver he calls "the peacemaker" at his side in a holster that looks like something a guy in the Old West would use. His daddy sent it to him, and he gets ammo in the mail every month or so. It's not regulation, but we're recon, so nobody really cares what we carry. "Heh, LT, look what we got!" He calls across the square to the LT who appears to be done with his transmission. "We gonna do some killin' tonight with these bad boys!" Poole's all pumped up, but the LT's looking a bit more dubious.

"You got ammo for those things?" he asks as he crosses over to the jeep. Poole looks into the back of the vehicle.

"Sure do. Let's take 'em down the road and check 'em out." They're new toys and so's everybody's interested as Poole unwraps the other three. But they're more interested in the LT and what we're gonna be doing later. Kids are standing around the jeep and look as excited as Poole.

"Sounds like a plan," the LT says. "Let's head down to the main. Take 'em to the field and fire 'em some. You know how to use them?" The LT picks one of the shotguns up and inspects it. He don't know a lot about firearms, him being from the East Coast and all, but he's game. "Close up your MEDCAP, Dreamy. We gotta go." Down the road we go in the three jeeps and park on the side of the road. Some gooks are coming in from the fields off to the left, and the sun is going down. We line up; I take one, Dreamy takes one, Shakes takes one, and Poole gives us a class in how to load 'em. "See, here, you load 'em from the side, seven rounds and one in the chamber. Here's the safety. Point and shoot. They got shells with little steel balls that scatter pretty good up to a range of fifty feet. My daddy had one of these."

"Fuck that," Thompson says after some thought. "I'm keepin' my thump gun. You never know when you gonna need some rounds downrange." Thompson was an expert with his M79 grenade launcher; he liked the size—it was short—and the fact that he was the only one in the platoon who could heave a grenade seventy-five meters out there with real accuracy. Of course, he didn't have an M16 to fire if he ran out of shells, but he always carried two bags of grenades and a .45 pistol. He was a short, stocky kid with a big wide back, and he didn't mind humping the extra weight. Anyway, when I fire the shotgun, it blows up, all fire and noise. There's not a lot of recoil, but the shell scatters part of a fence right in front of us. It's pretty impressive, and I'm in. Now's we're checked out, Poole divvies up the ammo and we put our M16s in the back of the jeep. We commence to opening up the C rats and we all give our peaches to Dreamy, who is crazy about them. As we're eating, the LT makes a sort of map on the back of a C rat box. We hand the spiced pork to the mice, who eat off to the side.

They don't speak much English and look like they're just hopin' to get through the night without any trouble. They got big steel helmets on, M16s, and ammo belts. But they don't look like they really know how to use them, so they get ignored as we listen to the LT.

"The police chief says five or ten dinks are coming in from the North, here through this field. Here's the rice factory we saw yesterday and the hootches across the street. There's the field just behind the factory, and here's the alley. Me, Poole, Shakes, and the two white mice will set up here, down the alley looking at the field. Thompson and Dreamy will set up across the street, covering our ass. You gonna set up claymores along the road so nobody gets behind us." He's pointing at me, so I know to gather up a couple of extra claymores before we get started. I'm gonna set up with Thompson and Dreamy to the rear. If all goes well, we won't have to do much, and I'm fine with that. "You'll be looking into the road and down the alley where we are. Hopefully, we blow the ambush, and you guys can come on over and help us clean up." Again, he points at me. "You got the one radio, and Shakes, you carry the other." Shakes don't say much. He's used to carrying the PRC25 for the LT and doing what he's told. He nods his head. "Make sure the batteries work," he mumbles. Shakes has got a Purple Heart from his time with Charlie Company and only really gets loud when he's drunk. Otherwise, it's clear he's just puttin' in his time. He would be happy if nothing happened tonight or any other night for that matter. But he's efficient, never complains, and goes with the flow. You gotta' respect that.

We drive the jeeps up the road to the police compound just off of the square. It's got some local cops inside, and they know not to mess with our stuff because we've been there before, and the chief told them to leave us alone. They stay inside the compound at night so they don't have to tangle with the VC, and the VC know to leave them alone. We smoke some as we wait for it to get dark. We tape down our gear and put some camouflage paint on our faces and hands, button up our shirts, and check our ammo. The shotguns feel funny because they don't have straps to hold on to, and I wish I had my trusty M16. Too late. And then out we go. Poole goes first, then the LT and Shakes. The mice are behind them and then there's Thompson, Dreamy, and me bringing up the rear. It's pretty quiet now. Everybody's inside their hootches and we assume they all know we're out and about. There's kerosene lamps lit, but mostly it's dark as hell. Inky dark, like you can't see your hand or your feet when you look down. Like a bag's been put over your head and you've been stuck in a closet. So dark that if you didn't have other senses you would begin to wonder if you really exist at all. Scary dark. The LT takes us to the left of the road, slowly. Every now and then he stops, and we all get down on our knees. We listen for sounds that are out of the ordinary, and then we move on. This is the bad part, the part I always hate. The moving around in the dark, waiting to walk into an ambush. The not-knowing-what's-gonna-happen part. I'm sopping wet with sweat, but my mind's on fire. All tuned up, listening for anything that tells me where the little people are. When I get down on my knees, I land on some rocks that dig into my kneecap. But I don't move. No noise, especially from us, is good noise. We move again and then Poole puts up his hand. I can't see him, but I can feel Dreamy go down on his knee and so I go down again. We're looking out, Dreamy to the left, me to the right. I'm also looking behind us to make sure nobody's following along. But I can't see anything and have to rely on my other senses. I'm whiffing for a smell, listening for any movement. Feeling to see if the air is moving different than before. It's all good so far. There's a thought banging in my head that I really don't need this shit. I need to be outta here and back home on the block, eating ice cream and chasing girls under lamplight, after supper, maybe, out with my mom. But I scoot the thought away and smell some more.

Then, as we are walking, Dreamy points to the left; the three of us—Thompson, Dreamy, and I—move off the road into the front yard of a hootch. Poole, the LT, Shakes, and the mice are gone, but Dreamy points out the alley to me. We lay down in a line along the road facing the rice factory and the alley on the other side. Thompson goes to check out the hootch, and I commence to setting up four claymores out near the road. I place them in front of some piles of dirt so's the blowback don't hit us, and I run the wires back to where Dreamy is down on the ground. I hand him the clackers, and he puts them in front of him. Dreamy's in charge of our little crowd, so he's gonna decide when to use the claymores. It's all done without any talking. We can see a little bit better now; our night vision is pretty good, at least as far as movement is concerned. I can't see Dreamy 'cause he's real black, but I can smell him. He's in a space five to ten feet to my left. I assume Thompson is on his left the other way. And then we wait.

First I'm hearin' a chicken moving around behind us, then a pig grunts. Later somebody is comforting a baby who is crying down the road. And then quiet again. The LT's set up down the alley looking out into the field. He's got the rice factory on his left, and there's a little space between it and another shed on his left as well. On the right is an old barn but there aren't any animals inside—more for storage, he figures. The factory is a big old structure—clapboard with a high peaked roof. He's got claymores out into the field, Poole's shotgun, Shake's shotgun, three M16s counting the mice's, grenades, and a bunch of pistols. He knows we're behind him, down the alley and across the street. He's hearing nothing. He calls in to me, "Danger Six Alpha, Danger Six Alpha." He whispers, "Sitrep, over."

I'm happy the radio is working, but his words seem like they're coming over a loud speaker. "Danger Six, this is Six Alpha." I'm whispering so low I can hardly hear myself. "Sitrep normal." I'm hoping he's got nothing else to say. The situation report is as normal as it's gonna get. And we all go quiet, hiding in the darkness and silence.

Well, of course, we wait a couple of hours, and it's nice and quiet. I'm beginning to think nothing is going to happen; the town's asleep, and it's about midnight. Even though I thought I was awake, a rock hits me in the head and I get startled. Dreamy's telling me to get my shit together. Down the road from the left come a line of dinks, single file like they was on some kinda parade. Most are holding their AKs, but some have them strapped to their backs. They're not saying anything, but you can hear 'em comin', and it's clear they don't think we're around. I can't see 'em all, but the line don't end as they pass Thompson, then Dreamy, and then me. "Holy shit," I'm thinkin'. And then it starts. Dreamy pulls on the clackers and three, then four claymores go off. A bunch of gooks go down right there in the street, but there's more, and they start yellin'. "Call it in," Dreamy screams. "Danger Six, this is Six Alpha. We got gooks on the road, maybe ten, maybe more, over." I drop the receiver and lift my shotgun up over the little berm in front of me and fire it. The recoil seems worse than before, probably because I'm layin' down. It scatters out onto the road and two more dinks go down, screaming since I shot 'em in the legs. But firing the round creates a big light out the end of the gun, and I notice that there're no flash suppressors on these weapons. I fire another round to my right, hoping to get any guys who might have made it past me, but the flash is so bright that I lose my night vision and pretty much telegraph my position. Gooks start shooting at where the light comes from, and I roll over a few feet closer to Dreamy. Problem is, Dreamy's making the same kinda light and is receiving a lot of fire every time he sets his gun off. "These guns is bad," he screams. "We can't use 'em!" We both shuffle to our left to near where Thompson is located and pull out our .45s. The rounds are coming pretty hot and heavy, since there appear to be dinks down the road to the right and up the road to our left.

"Six Alpha, this is Six. You guys OK? Over." The LT's firing down the alley, and the rounds are going over our heads. We see the tracers and try to stay real low. Dreamy throws a grenade down the road that explodes, but there's no screaming.

"So far, so good," I scream into the box. There's all kind of yelling in gook, and some guy's got a bugle he's blowing. We can hear them backing up the road and going toward the other side of the factory. "Sounds like they're heading your way, other side of the factory," I yell. And then an RPG goes screaming down the alleyway to where the LT is located. It crashes into something and explodes. More noise and more light. Claymores go off in the field in front of the LT's position, and there's some screaming. Somebody got hit. But now there's screaming all around us; somebody's giving orders down the road to my right, up the road to my left, behind the rice factory, and in the field. The bugle's blaring, and Poole's shotgun goes off—more light, more return fire, another claymore goes off, and the AKs are rattling. There's clearly a lot more dinks than we thought. We're getting surrounded.

"Alpha." Poole comes across the radio. "LT's down. Got blown up from that RPG. We can't use the guns. You keep firin' up the road. We're gonna keep 'em off of us with grenades!" He's huddled near that little space between where the factory ends and the shed begins. A gook starts shooting through the space, and Poole throws a grenade in there, which blows the shit out of the clapboard and seems to discourage the dink. But they seem like they're every-where, shootin' and yellin', the bugle blowin' and RPGs goin' off. Shakes is grabbing grenades out of his pocket and pulling the pins. He stands up, throws a grenade onto the roof of the factory, and lets it roll down the other side. He's wary though. If he misses, the grenade's gonna roll back down on his side of the factory into the alley and blow him away. The mice are in the corner of the alley, not doing much, and the LT's layin' on the ground.

All this goes on for a while but then settles down. The gooks are moving around, firing some but mostly trying to figure out exactly where we are and how many of us there are. Thompson's throwing grenades down the road, but he can't get a real good shot. Poole kneels down next to the LT and checks to see if he's alive. The LT's got shrapnel wounds all over his face and arm, but there're no sucking chest wounds and no big gashes anywhere along his extremities. He's kinda smilin' as he lays there all crashed out. "Shit," Poole mumbles. "LT, you all right?" Nothing. "LT, you gotta' get up now. We need your weapon. Time for you to get us outta this shit." Nothing. Poole stands up and kicks the LT. "Wake the fuck up, goddamn it!"

The LT comes out of whatever dream he's in and looks at Poole. "OK," he says. "What's goin' on?" Later he tells us he could hear Poole yelling at him but didn't want to wake up. He thought he was dead and was kind of relieved that he didn't have to be responsible for the shit-storm that was going on around us. He said he was just watching it all as he drifted above us and didn't want to come back.

Poole reaches over and grabs another grenade. The little people are out in the field and on the other side of the factory. He pulls the pin and rolls it down the roof to where they're all hootin'. After the blast, the yellin' stops but the bugle keeps blaring. Except for the tracers, it's so dark we can't see shit, especially the dinks as they move around. 'N', of course, by now we've figured out that there's a lot more of them than there are of us. "Get on the horn, 'n' get us some help. We need some more people out here," Poole says, as he checks the space between the factory and the shed. He picks up the LT's M16 and fires a burst. "Shakes? You OK?" he yells.

From down the alley near the open field, Shakes answers, "Yeah, but the shotguns is fucked. The mice aren't doing much. Mebbe we can use their M16s." He throws another grenade into the field. "How long we plannin' on staying here?"

"Beats the shit out of me," Poole answers. "LT, you gotta do something. There's a lot of dinks out there, and we can't see shit. Boys across the road are all right for now, but there's no way we move 'em over here...What you think?"

The LT grabs the radio mike and calls into battalion. He's wiping blood off his face and checking the rest of his body to see if there are any other wounds. One of his eyes is shut, and he can't tell if he's shot there or if it's just blood from his head.

"Darkness Six, this is Danger Six, over." A Chicom grenade comes crashing over the fence between the alley and the open field. Everybody ducks for cover, and the blast travels over their heads.

"Shit," Shakes mumbles. "Heh, you guys!" He grabs one of the mice by the ammo belt and moves him to the fence looking out on the open field. "You shoot there," he says, and points. "I shoot here." He points to the factory. "You got it?" The mouse looks up at him like he don't understand. "You shoot." Shakes points to the field. "Bang-bang!" He grabs the M16, points it at the field, and fires off a clip. "Now you!" The mouse is real young and real scared, but he looks like he understands and pulls another clip from his belt and starts to fire. Shakes goes back to the wall of the factory and commences throwing grenades over the roof. "Shit, can't see nothin'," he mumbles. A grenade comes over the fence from the open field and explodes. The LT is seated with his back to the fence up the alley and gets hit again. "Damn!" he yells. "That hurts!" Shakes moves over to the mouse and sees him laying flat; a portion of his ear and forehead is gone. He's alive but stunned and moaning. "One down here," Shakes tells the LT over his shoulder, and proceeds to pull a bandage from his belt and wrap it around the wounded man's head. "Sonsabitches!" He finishes and reaches around to find the other mouse, who is huddled in the brush. "Now your turn, cocksucker...You shoot 'em up! Go bang-bang!" he says, and points at the field. Shakes is so pissed the dink can smell the rage on him and starts to fire into the field. He's clearly more afraid of Shakes than he is of the bad guys.

"Danger Six, this is Darkness Six. Sitrep, over," the battalion answers.

"This is Danger Six. Presently surrounded with a force of maybe thirty or so. Some enemy KIA, one wounded Vietnamese cop. We're running out of ammo, and the enemy has got us surrounded, over!"

"What do you need, Danger Six?"

"What do we need?" The LT is all but screaming now. He's clearly tuned up, maybe in shock, but all engines are roarin'.

Battalion comes on again. "Calm down, Danger Six. What do you need?"

The LT gets the message. He's talking to the battalion commander and not making much sense. His training, or something, kicks in. "I am going to need reinforcements. We only got six of us out here. But more than that we need light. Lots of illumination so's we can see the little bastards!" He swivels to the right and fires a burst of M16 rounds through the space between the factory and the shed, as he watches Poole calmly rolling grenades down the roof of the building.

"Can't give you artillery illumination, Danger Six. No artillery allowed inside a ville. Tends to start fires, over."

"Fires!" the LT screams to himself. He's not transmitting now and thinks he's talking to himself. "I don't give a shit if you get a battalion out here with flashlights. I need illumination now!"

"What was that, Danger Six?" The battalion commander is pissed. He don't like getting yelled at by lieutenants, even if they are in a fire fight.

"Uh, yeah, Darkness Six. We gonna need some light. Mebbe you can fire to the North, just outside the ville. That might help. A gunship for sure and some reinforcements. I'm hit as well," he adds, "but not bad, over."

"OK, Danger Six, we'll get on it and get back to you. Stay calm and out of trouble. Out." Now the yelling is coming from the other side of the factory. One guy sounds like he's giving orders. The bugle's still going and there's a lot of crashing through the field. You could feel the noose tightening, as the gooks get closer. They're in the field and just on the other side of the factory. Can't be more than twenty feet away. Some guy sticks his head into the space between the factory and shed and fires off some rounds. It's only a few feet away from Poole and the LT. "Sonofabitch!" Poole screams. He pulls a pin and throws the grenade into the space. The explosion is right on top of them as well, and they get hit with flying wood from the walls of the factory. The LT looks around. "Nice," he mutters.

"Danger Six Alpha, you there? Over." No answer. That can't be good, and the LT tries again. "Danger Six Alpha, pick up the fuckin' phone, over!" I'm kinda busy at that point. I hear the LT over the mike, but it's laying on the ground and I can't see it. As I'm fumbling around, Thompson throws another grenade down the road at an angle. It sort of hits the corner of the factory, and we hear a guy scream. "Gotcha, you sonofabitch!" I find the phone.

"Six, this is Alpha, over."

"What's going on over there? You guys OK? Over." I look around and see Dreamy firing his .45. There don't seem to be any more gooks in the road, so's it looks like the LT's ass is covered, at least that part that is exposed by the alley.

"Six, this is Alpha. I think we're OK," I say with relief. "They seem to be comin' at you 'n' leavin' us alone, over." I keep looking to my right to see if there's any more down that way, but nothing's moving.

"OK." The LT pauses. "We're kinda busy here. You guys stay where you are. We got illumination and a gunship coming in. Reinforcements on the way. Stay cool, and don't use up your ammo. It's gonna be a while, out." And that's what we do. We keep an eye on the alley so's no more gooks can fire down it; Thompson throws some grenades at the corner of the factory and the road, and we go silent. Dreamy moves us just a little bit to the left and tells me to keep my eye on the right side of the road. He's gonna' look at our rear where the hootches are, and Thompson is covering the left side of the road.

Seems like forever, but after a while, some illum comes bursting over the area north of us outside the ville. The little parachutes float out and over the hootches, making lots of shadows along the road. Then there's a gunship firing some kind of Gatling gun into the field north of us. It spits lots of rounds and sounds real dangerous. We're hopin' it don't get too close and blow us away. The gooks are still moving around trying to get an angle on us. The LT, Poole, and Shakes are still dropping grenades over the roof of the factory.

There's some screams, but mostly they're just keeping the gooks at bay. The LT takes a position between the factory and the shed and is firing his M16 into the dark.

The radio crackles and I hear somebody trying to get a hold of the LT. "Danger Six, this is Dagger Six, over." The LT don't answer, and I'm trying to remember who Dagger Six is. "Danger Six, this is Dagger Six, over." After a while, the LT comes on the net, and I can hear him and all the firing behind him as he talks.

"This is Danger Six, over."

"Dagger Six, what you got? Over."

The LT is still pumped but answers real clear. "We got thirty gooks surrounding us at north end of ville. Two wounded and running out of ammo. Where you at? Over."

"We're on the main. Is the road up to the ville clear? I don't want my tracks to get blown up, over."

"Clear?" I'm thinkin'. There's gooks all around us. We're in Vietnam, the Republic of, for Christ's sakes. There's nothin' clear until you get your ass on a big bird and go the fuck back to the world. I wanna scream at the lieutenant sonofabitch, but I know better.

"Clear enough, I'm thinkin'," says the LT. "We were on it this evening. No mines then, over."

"OK, we're on our way up. When I get close, you pop some flares. Otherwise we're gonna blow away anything we see, over." Of course, that can't be good. I mean, three armored personnel carriers—tracks—with M50 machine guns and M60 machine guns, plus troops with M16s, thump guns, and grenades. The carriers don't normally come into villes at night, and they make great targets. Only thing worse than VC is scared GIs with firepower.

The LT checked in with battalion. "Darkness Six, this is Danger Six. You copy my last with Dagger Six? Over." Poole dives into the space between the factory and the shed and throws two grenades, one to the left and one to the right. He ducks back into the alley and waits. The bugle continues to blow as the grenades go off.

"That should hold 'em," Poole mutters. "Shakes, how's the field lookin'?" The mouse has now fired all his rounds. Shakes got two more grenades left and a pistol.

"Gimme two of the LT's magazines. We're outta rounds here." He's fumbling with one of the shotguns but can't figure out how to load it in the dark. "Poole, next time you decide to change weapons on us, leave me out!" He throws the gun on the ground and reaches for the magazines. He jerks the M16 out of the mouse's hand and reloads it. He fires a short burst where he thinks some gooks might be and looks down at the wounded cop. "This one's startin' to bleed out pretty fast. We gonna' need a medevac pretty quick, LT."

"Got it! Darkness Six, Danger Six. Did you copy my last with Dagger Six? Over." There's less AK firing now, but the illums are still coming over the ville, and the gunship is shooting up the countryside outside of town.

"Roger Danger Six, Dagger Six on the way, over." Things are coming together.

"Darkness Six, I'm gonna need a medevac for one wounded IP, shot in the head and bleeding pretty bad, over." The LT hands Poole two grenades. "That's my last two. Think it's gonna be a while longer."

And then it's over. The bugle stops, the AKs cease firing, and there's a shit-load of silence. There's nothing but Gatling gun bursts a long way off and popping illums making shadows. It's eerie.

"Alpha, you still on the line, over?" The LT checks with me, and his voice is low and cracked. Drink some water, I'm thinking.

"Roger, Six, we're here and it's all good, over."

"Look, the quarter cav is coming up the road right about now. They should be in the square in titi time. Stay put or you're gonna get your ass shot off. When I tell you, pop a flare out into the middle of the road and wait some more. I'll tell you what to do, over." The LT stands up and stretches.

"Get the fuck down, LT!" Poole screams. "This shit ain't done yet." The LT gets down and waits until we hear the tracks come lumbering up the road. They're moving fast but not firing at anything. They got little green lights on in the front. Poole lights a cigarette, and the LT shares it with him.

"Dagger Six, this is Danger Six. We see you. We're puttin' out a flare. Don't know if there's still gooks around, but tell your guys not to fire us up, over."

"OK, we're ready, over." The lieutenant in the track has a high-pitched voice. He sounds kinda scared, and that is not very encouraging. The hootches around us on both sides of the road are dark and silent. We're waitin' for some dinks to start firing at the tracks, and nobody wants to stand up. Suddenly, one of the M60s goes off and lights up a hootch behind Dreamy. And then another one fires into the factory, over the heads of the LT, Shakes, and Poole. My face is two inches into the rocks and dirt in front of me, and I'm tryin' to pull my ass into the hole with the rest of me.

"Stop firing, goddamn it, stop firing!" the LT screams into the phone. The M60s stop their noise, and we all listen to see if there are any AKs firing back. None.

"Alpha, this is Danger Six. Throw the flare, over." Thompson gets on his knees real slow; throws the flare out into the road; and then falls back down on his stomach, waiting for all hell to break loose.

"Got it," says Dagger Six. "Come on out." Right then, a medevac comes hovering overhead. The pilot is on the line as well.

"Danger Six, this is Robin Hood, over." The LT looks up. Another target for the VC to shoot at. "You got room for us to land and pick up your indigenous personnel? Looks like there's hootches on both sides. We gonna have enough room for our blades? Over." The LT low-crawls up the alley and peers out into the street. To his left, he sees three tracks down the road aways with a guy on an M60 aimed right at him. LT's holding on to the radio. Nobody wants to stand up 'cause there might be little people in the shadows of the hootches, and we're not real clear what the guy on the M60 is pre-pared to do. The white mice, especially the one who's not wounded, are scared shitless. They're the only dinks still left in this scenario, and they know better than to sneak around in the shadows with a lot of scared GIs just dying to light up the entire town.

"Poole, come up here," the LT whispers. "Bring the mice." Poole and Shakes low-crawl up the alley with the mice and stop. The wounded dink is groaning now, talkin' some "I'm gettin' ready to die" shit in Vietnamese. The LT takes his strobe light out of his pocket and checks to see if it works. Somebody's got to stand in the middle of the road and shine the light so's the mede-vac can land. "If I give you the thumbs up, you tell that pilot to come on in. If that M60 starts shooting, you blow that sonofabitch away. Got it?" Poole nods, although he's hard to see in the dark. The LT waits a real long minute. "Ah, fuck it."

The LT stands up. He grabs the wounded cop and cradles him over his shoulder. Then he grabs up the other one, puts his arm around him, and starts walking to the street. "Comin' out!" he yells...And most amazing of all, nobody, I mean nobody, shoots him down.

There's more to the story, of course. The pilot's able to get in, although it's close, and the mouse gets out. The gooks are all gone, and the guys from the tracks cover us as we all come out from under the shadows. When it's all over, the LT gets a medal and gets some shrapnel pulled out of his eye and back. Some big guy in black jungle fatigues shows up the next day and interro-gates us all, looks at the bodies of the dead gooks, and wanders off. We put the shotguns back in their cases and store them in the supply room back in Lai Khe. And nobody ever mentions them again.

CANTOR'S FAIRYTALE

PROLOGUE:

Sergeant Jake Cantor, recently graduated from a prestigious university in Washington DC, and a squad leader in the third platoon of Charlie Company, 2/18th Infantry, Second Brigade, First Infantry Division, Vietnam, Republic of, opened the door to the Quonset hut and saw nothing but black. There was a light at the end of the hut, a bar of sorts, and two signs on the far wall: one that read "BIG RED ONE, DUTY FIRST" and another that read "We Who are About to Die, Salute You." He paid no attention. Shit like that was on walls all over the rear area. He wanted a cold beer and a place to sit quietly and sleep. Cantor waited for his eyes to adjust and then stepped wearily in. This Quonset hut, after all, passed for an officer's club, and normally he would have no right to enter. But the first sergeant told him to go wait there until the chopper left for Vung Tau and his three-day R&R, and he guessed the first sergeant knew what he was talking about. Besides, he'd been pretty drunk for the last two days and had had a bad attitude—bad enough, he recognized, that he might look for somebody to hit or at least chew out. He knew it when the mood came over him and always tried to shut up and stay away from folks. Three more months and he would be out of this shit; just keep it clean and lay low, do your job, and go home. Cantor wasn't looking for any trouble and hoped none would find him, because he was too tired and too pissed off to care about what might happen. A beer, a nap, and two days on the beach—with those he might find the energy to get through the last round, keep his people alive, and maybe stay alive himself. That was enough...more than enough.

At the end of the hut, seated next to a jukebox, sat another man who was reading a book. At first look he didn't appear to be much different than Cantor—he had baggy jungle fatigues, unstarched and wrinkled; mud-stained boots with a hint that they had once been black and new; and a boonie hat bunched up on the table next to a can of beer. He wore a combat infantryman's badge stitched onto his shirt, a ranger tab, jump wings, and a long droopy moustache that went way below the sides of his lips. His hair was short but uncombed; his eyes were red, and his skin brown and blotchy. Another grunt, Cantor thought, and relaxed, until he noticed the first lieutenant bar on his collar. "OK," his mind calculated, "but a grunt nonetheless."

"Afternoon, Lieutenant," Cantor said. "First sergeant told me to come in here and wait for the bird to Vung Tau...Where you from?" The lieutenant looked up from his book and took a chug from his beer.

"Come on in," he said, looking Cantor over. The same boots, the same unstarched fatigues, the same vague uneasiness about being in the rear with all the regulations. How to act? They both knew it was the lieutenant's job to set the rules and define how the next few hours would go. If the lieutenant wanted to be a prick he could send Cantor out of the club, and he would have to spend the next few hours sitting in the shade of the building waiting for the plane. Cantor waited. "There's beer behind the bar there and some pretzels. Get you some if you like. First sergeant told me to wait in here as well. Seems we're all goin' to Vung Tau in a couple of hours. I'm Bobbie Knight from the recon platoon. Who you been walkin' with?"

Cantor walked to the bar and reached into the cooler for a beer. "You want a beer?" he asked.

"Sure enough," Knight answered. "Keep 'em comin'."

Cantor grabbed two beers and two bags of pretzels and walked over to the lieutenant's table. "Here you go, LT. I'm with the third herd of Charlie Company. We been up in the Parrot's Beak and up and down Thunder Road. What they have you guys doin?"

Knight motioned for Cantor to sit down and lit a cigarette from a plastic case on the table. "We been doing LRRPs up along the border for a while. Ain't seen nothin' though. Been pretty quiet."

"How short?" Knight asked, as Cantor settled into the chair across from him, put his cigarettes on the table, and pulled his book out of his cargo pants.

"Ninety-eight days and a wake-up," Cantor answered. "You?"

"Hunert 'n' thirty-five," Knight answered. "Where you from?" Knight looked lonely and kind of agitated, Cantor noticed. He also looked kind of drunk. Maybe Cantor wasn't going to get a nap after all.

"I'm from New Jersey and then DC. School and stuff, you know? You?"

"Georgia's my home. Columbus, around Benning. You ever been there?"

"Yeah." Cantor sighed, remembering his training at the Noncommissioned Officer Academy there. "Went to shake 'n' bake school at Benning…Got to say there are no great memories."

Knight chuckled. "Yeah, I kin understand that. Went to OCS there myself." They both drifted off for a moment into thoughts of that dusty fort with its "HOME OF THE INFANTRY" signs and 3.2 beer. "Not much to recommend it…Seems like a long time ago." Knight got up and went behind the bar. "You wanna 'nother beer?" He pulled two out of the cooler and came around the bar before Cantor could answer. "At least this shit's cold," Knight muttered as he sat down.

"You know," Knight said, as he lit another cigarette; his first one was still in the ashtray burning down. "I knew a guy from Charlie Company." He paused, thinking. "Nun…yeah…Charlie Nun." Knight smiled and popped the top off his beer can. "Old Nun. Nun o' this 'n' nun o' that, thank you." Knight laughed to himself. "Couldn't shine a pair o' boots to save his ass. He was gone the first month. Know him?"

Cantor shrugged one of those Vietnam "don't mean nothin'" shrugs, and looked away from Knight's eyes and into his beer can. He listened to the whirl of the air conditioner, blasting on overload at the other end of the hut, until the door suddenly opened and a shard of light assaulted his pupils. Blinded, both he and Knight looked away. In walked a short, skinny, black kid with nappy hair and cruddy boots. "Another grunt lost in the rear," Cantor thought. The kid knew he was in officer country and had his guard up. "First sergeant tol' me to come 'n' here 'n' wait till the plane goin' to Vung Tau," he announced, so nobody would think he was an intruder.

Knight was the gatekeeper. He said, "Come on in, and shut the goddamn door...You're lettin' all the air out. Beer's cold, costs a dime." He lit another cigarette. Almost immediately a third man opened the door and peered inside, unable to see because of the darkness.

"Damn, this is turnin' into a party," said Knight. "This here's the waitin' room for the Vung Tau express. 'Pears we're all on a journey... Buncha pilgrims looking for salvation at the beach. Set yourself down 'n' have a beer. Grab me one while you're at it!" Cantor watched the skinny black kid behind the bar. "He can't be eighteen," he thought. The other guy was bigger, much bigger, with blond hair all over his tanned arms and a balding brown head.

They were all seated at the same table, which by now had a number of empty cans and full ashtrays. They exchanged the usual pleasantries, and everyone established what company they were with, how short they were, and where they'd done their training in the states. The black kid turned out to have a high-pitched voice, a bit of a lisp, and a New York accent. His name was Lucifer Jenkins, and he was in the army all of seven months. Seems, before he joined up at seventeen, he had never been out of Harlem. Apparently he'd gotten into a jam with the police and they gave him a choice: six months in jail or two years in the army.

The other guy was from Minnesota and mumbled his name, Stephan. "But everybody calls me Swede," he noted, as Knight started making a pyramid out of the beer cans.

That done, and with an officer at the table, there was a lull in the conversation. More beer and cigarettes. Lucifer was getting drunk pretty fast. "They say you can get laid pretty good down in Vung Tau. Guys gave me some money and tol' me to go for it. Is that true, Lieutenant?"

"Sho' enough, but you gotta watch out, young stud. You come back with the clap 'n' have to stay out of the field for a couple of days, your First Shirt will kick your ass. That's a fact." Knight started laughing, and Cantor and the Swede joined in. Lucifer looked confused. Clearly he wasn't going to Vung Tau to sit on the beach, and yet they all were pretty sure he'd never been with a woman before.

"Stick with girls at the hotel," Swede said, talking to no one in particular. "They get checked out by the medics so's there's no problems. That's what I'm gonna do." Everybody nodded, recognizing the wisdom of it all, and Lucifer relaxed.

Another lull. Like most grunts, they were five minutes away from falling asleep where they sat if nothing was going on. Knight jumped up and went to the bar for four more beers. As he returned he announced, "Looks like we got some time to kill here. Got a game for you young killers. Each of us tells a story, somethin' they seen or done in the bush. Then we all vote, 'n' the one with the best tale gets that bottle of gin sittin' on the bar. I'll buy it!" Of course this wasn't an order, but it did come from Knight, who was an officer.

"What the fuck," Swede murmured. "I'm in if you guys are." He was looking at Cantor to see if there might be a trap somehow.

"Sure," Cantor laughed. "Why not?" Nobody asked Lucifer, but they assumed he would go along. "Swede, why don't you go first?" Knight suggested. Swede pulled a Tiparillo from his chest pocket, lit it up with his Zippo lighter, and took a long drink from his beer can. He blew some smoke across the room and started to talk.

SWEDE'S TALE:

"There was this guy named Esposito in my platoon when I got there. He'd been in the bush a long time; I think he extended six months so's he could get an early out, and everybody was pretty sure he had his shit together. I mean, he didn't carry nothin' extra in his ruck, but he always had what you needed—extra batteries; a needle 'n' thread; his poncho, of course; pogey bait crackers 'n' such; a toothbrush to clean his weapons and one to brush his teeth; a book to read; extra matches in plastic bags; a wash cloth 'n' soap; extra socks; bug repellant; 'n' rubbers to put over the tip of his weapon. I mean, most us had some of that shit, but we always carried lots more stuff until we learned better. He had extra ammo, grenades, a real sharp machete, 'n' a .45, which the lieutenant let him keep, 'cause frankly nobody fucked with Esposito, even if he was only a spec four.

"Now, he was in charge of a special squad of mostly black guys they called the Buffalo Scouts. They had all been around awhile and always walked point. Said they didn't want some rookie new boots walkin' them into no ambush. They slept in their own bunker in the rear, partied by themselves, didn't haf to do no shit details, 'n' set up their own ambushes in the woods. It wasn't racial or nothin' like that, just the old guys watchin' out for each other. 'N' Esposito was in charge.

"One day, we're bustin' bush for the company, and the Buffalo Scouts are walkin' point. We get the word to hold up, 'n' we all get down in the mud. It's hot like always, and even though it's only ten hundred hours, the bugs are out in droves. Next thing I know, a grenade goes off up front. Course I can't see shit, but I see the lieutenant get up and walk up the trail to where Esposito is. He tells the lieutenant that there's a gook up ahead settin' booby traps with trip wires, so's we got to go slow. We walk a bit farther, looking for gooks in the trees or down along a small stream on our right, and then another grenade goes off. This time a kid named Melvin Johnson tripped a wire. He's layin' on the side of the trail with half his leg blown off 'n' the doc is bandaging him up. He's screaming pretty loud, and the lieutenant calls a medevac.

We grab him up, some of us guys in the rear of the platoon, and hand-carry his ass with a poncho out to a field, and the medevac comes in and takes him away. Meanwhile, Esposito's flippin' out. He's screamin' up the trail, 'You little gook bastard! I'm comin' to get you! You little fuck!' The lieutenant's tryin' to calm him down, and then the platoon sergeant comes up and gets in Esposito's face.

"'Esposito, shut the fuck up. If you can't do your job, we're gonna put you in the back of the platoon, and you can walk trail for a while.' Esposito calms down 'n' says he's ready to go…Don't mean nothin', 'n' all that shit. Back up the trail he stomps, 'n' off we go. Course everyone's scared now…I mean, we're lookin' for trip wires on the ground, the trees, across the trail, for ambushes and every other kinda shit. Nothin' for about half an hour. Then we get a hand signal from the lieutenant to halt. He heads up the trail and then comes back to me and another guy named Franklin, and he tells us to head up the file till we see Esposito and cover for him.

"When we get up there, Esposito is all quiet and whispering. He points to the right and says there's a bunker down by the stream and that the gook and maybe his buddies are hidin' in it. Well, let me tell you, I'm not a happy trooper. I'm sweatin' so hard I can hardly see, Esposito is all excited, 'n' Franklin's not sayin' a word. Down we go in the mud and level our 16s at the stream. Esposito takes off his ruck, puts his 16 down on top so's it won't get dirty, and crawls toward the bunker with his .45 'n' a bunch a grenades. When he hits the bunker, after what seems like an hour, he crawls around to one side and stands up. Then he points at us so's we know to light it up once he's out of the way. In go the grenades—one, then two. Esposito takes off.

"Esposito is runnin' back toward us when one of the grenades goes off. No big thing; the explosion's inside the bunker. But then all hell breaks loose. The bunker blows up, sideways, and through the top like there's an arsenal inside. Metal's flyin' everywhere, and I'm keeping my head real low until I see Esposito's body come cartwheelin' by me in the air like some kinda' doll. I crawl back to where he lands, sure he's double dead, and I'm lookin' over his body for blood 'n' wounds. But there's nothin'—no blood, no holes, even though Esposito is stone-cold out.

"The lieutenant and the rest of the platoon come runnin' up the trail and head down toward what's left of the bunker. Turns out there were three gooks in there and enough ammunition and C4 to blow us all away. The platoon secures the area, the lieutenant is talkin' to the captain, and Esposito wakes up. He checks his nuts and legs. 'Got that fucker,' he says, cool as can be. 'Anybody got a cigarette?'"

Nobody's saying much around the table, until Knight gets up and gets more beers. "That's a pretty good story, Swede," he says. "Whatever happened to Esposito? He get home all right?"

"Naw…well, maybe," Swede mutters. "Last week he was bustin' bush with that machete of his. It slipped and cut a huge slice off his leg. Heard he got medevac'd to Japan for some surgeries."

"Damn," Cantor said, and they all shook their heads. "Bummer."

Knight seemed to wake everyone up. "OK, Lucifer, your turn."

LUCIFER'S TALE:

Lucifer's a little nervous, but he's also pretty drunk. "Wow," he starts. "Never seen nothin' like that. I only been in-country six weeks. They keep me right behind Platoon Sergeant Miller, the platoon sergeant. I carry his radio and do what he tells me. We're in the back most of the time, and the lieutenant is up front…But there is this one guy.

"Doc is our medic, and he's from Mississippi. They tell me that because he's from down South, he don't like Negros. I don't know about that. Anyway, he's a funny kinda fella, 'cause he refuses to carry a weapon or shoot at anyone. He's always reading the Bible while the rest of us are setting up ambushes—you know, putting out claymores, figuring out where to shoot if somebody comes down a trail, getting our flares ready. Mostly, I'm talking to the company, doing my commo checks while all that's going on, and Doc is just sitting there next to me, reading his Bible. When the sun is down, he puts his Bible away and says his prayers. He says 'em out loud, but real low, and nobody seems to mind. His big thing to do is make sure everybody takes his malaria pills. If somebody gets cut on the trail, he bandages him up, and he's always checking our feet. Some of the guys get the rot real bad. I had it when I first got here, and it sucks. You know, raw meat, scabs, bloody toes. All o' that. He's allays making us take off our boots and change our socks. 'N' he checks everybody's feet real slow, gets his hands right into all that blood 'n' pus 'n' cleans them up real good. If somebody's got the rot bad, he argues with the lieutenant about sending him to the rear to dry out. Most of the guys don't want to go, but he's real strict 'n' makes 'em get on the chopper. Still, seems crazy to be out in the woods without a weapon. I asked him once about it, 'n' he says Jesus is watching over him, so's he don't need no gun. Besides, the commandments tell him not to kill no one. When I come into the army, my momma told me that Jesus would be watching out for me too. But I should do what I was told, and learn how to shoot so's I could come home to her. I'm thinkin' that was real good advice.

"Anyway, a couple of weeks ago, we was on ambush after humpin' all day up near Thunder Road. I made my commo checks and settled down next to Platoon Sergeant Miller. Sure enough, Doc was saying his prayers and then I was off to sleep. Around two in the morning, Platoon Sergeant Miller wakes me up for my two-hour shift. I sit up and start to look down this little hill we're on. The stars are out, and all kinda animals are chirpin' 'n' hootin' in the bushes. I'm kind of lonely, but I'm tryin' to do what Platoon Sergeant Miller told me to do. If I see or hear anything, I should wake him up immediately, so's he can alert the rest of the platoon and fire off the claymores.

"Don't you know, after a while I hear a bunch of guys comin' down the trail like they was in the St. Patrick's Day parade. I mean, they're laughin' and carrying on like there's nobody else in the woods, and they're heading home for dinner. I go to wake up Platoon Sergeant Miller, but he's already awake and tapping the guy next to him. He's a big white fellow from Tennessee, and he's tapping the guy next to him. Next thing I know, the claymores go off, and everybody is shooting down the hill. We got flares and grenades, thump guns, and M16 fire all going down the hill at the Viet Cong. Those Viet Cong soldiers never had a chance. When the lieutenant tells us to stop, it's pretty quiet, but some of those guys are moanin' down below. We're all kind of afraid they might still be lookin' to shoot back at us, so we're stayin' real low. And then Doc stands up. 'Anybody hurt?' he asks. Nobody answers. 'I've got to go treat the wounded, Lieutenant. Tell everybody to be cool.' 'N' off he goes. Platoon Sergeant Miller mutters somethin' like 'Ah, shit,' and follows him down the hill. Of course, even though I don't want to, I got to follow Platoon Sergeant Miller wherever he goes, so I put on my radio and head down the hill after them.

"On the trail, there's four guys who are blown up. I mean, one's got no mouth to speak of; another's missing an arm. A third guy is bleeding all over the trail and trying to crawl away, but he's missing both his legs and his guts are trailing behind him. I'm feeling like I'm gonna puke, but I'm keeping my eye on Platoon Sergeant Miller, who is searching everybody for weapons…Doc is kneeling next to a fourth guy who has some kind of wound in the chest. He's having a hard time breathing. Doc gives him a shot of something and then puts a plastic bag over his chest, which seems to help him breathe. He checks the other guys and then says to the lieutenant, who has gotten the rest of the platoon to surround the area, 'We need a medevac for two wounded. Gotta have it now.' Silversmith, the lieutenant's RTO, calls back, and after a while we put the two wounded Viet Cong on a chopper.

"Course it's a couple hours before dawn now. The lieutenant moves the platoon down the trail a ways and sets up for the rest of the night. Platoon Sergeant Miller puts out more claymores, and doc lays down, says his prayers, and goes off to sleep. Just like that. Jesus, I'm thinkin' I never seen anything like it."

Cantor, Knight, and Swede all clap. It's clear to them that Lucifer isn't too bright and, of course, he's still real young. They all seem to understand how vulnerable the poor kid is and want him to know he's done well. By now, Knight is clearly drunk. He reaches for his beer and knocks over the pyramid. Everybody laughs, and Swede heads back to the bar.

KNIGHT'S TALE:

"I got to admit, there's days I miss bein' in a line platoon. I mean, on the upside, you got all those people around you when you're in the bush, plenty of firepower, two M60 machine guns, two grenade launchers, twenty or so M16s, a bunch of sergeants, and a couple of radios. There's definitely strength in numbers. On the other side, you livin' out in the mud 'n' rain for weeks at a time, the gooks know where you are 'cause you're makin' so much noise, 'n' if you don't watch it you kin get your ass kicked. That's why I didn't mind when they chose me to lead the recon platoon. Hell, mostly it's all good. Less time in the rain, better food for sure, 'n' a chance to really support the battalion. Eyes 'n' ears of the battalion 'n' all that. What I was trained for in ranger school. Course the last thing we want to do is get in a firefight, spring a bush and get in the shit.

"I been spendin' my time up near the Cambodian border with two other guys doing three-day recon missions. Know how that works? Well the point is to sit real quiet along the Ho Chi Mihn Trail 'n' see whose coming down it 'n' then report back to HQ. Mostly it's a lark; we sleep a lot, don't move around much, 'n' only use the radios twice a day. 'Cause, you know, there's no help comin' if they find you. It's quiet mostly, 'n' you want to keep it that way.

"This one time I'm working with a guy named Ploughman and a guy named Smith. Smith is my platoon sergeant; he's been in the Nam twice before and knows his way around. Ploughman is a new guy, and we're takin' him along to show him the ropes. I'm carrin' the PRC 25 'n' my M16, Smith's got a thump gun 'n' a 16, 'n' Ploughman's got a 16. We're all loaded up with grenades, and we've all got .45s. We got paint on our faces, some Korean C rats, two canteens each, no helmets, 'n' only poncho liners to sleep in. But that's about it. Battalion's forty klicks away, so we're kinda on our own. We head out on a chopper right around dawn—just the three of us, two door gunners, 'n' two pilots. First, the chopper gets real high as we travel north, up where the air is nice 'n' cool and there's no smell. We're all enjoyin' that when we start to descend into a landing zone. The gunners start to fire their 60s, and the chopper hits the dirt and then takes off. We don't dismount, 'cause we're just trying to confuse the gooks about where we are 'n' how many of us there is. We do this three more times, 'n' then the pilot tells us through the earphones, 'OK, guys, the next one's for real.'

"This time the M60s stay quiet, 'n' the chopper hovers 'bout five feet off the ground. Smith goes first, jumps, 'n' rolls in the dirt like we was landin' in jump school. Ploughman's next, and he don't roll; he tries to land straight up. I'm right behind him 'n' fall right on top of him. We both go down into the grass. Smith's already runnin' toward the woods 'n' cover, but when Ploughman gets up, he's gruntin', 'cause he screwed up his ankle. I grab a hold of him, and we hobble into the trees, hopin' nobody sees us. We make it into the nipa; nobody says nothin' 'n' we wait to see if any gooks come rollin' into the LZ. Nothin'. After about fifteen minutes, I make my commo check with battalion; nice to see at least they know where we are. Smith points at me, makes a sign off to the right, 'n' we start into the woods. Ploughman's hobblin' a bit but keepin' up. Smith finds a little break in the jungle where the animals travel, and we follow it for a while, all very slow and quiet-like. The farther we go, the darker it gets, 'cause the jungle is gettin' thick, but the trail is kinda clear so we don't have to make any noise bustin' bush. Smith stops every now and then to look at his map; he shows it to me 'n' then keeps on walkin'. We really need to know where we are 'cause if we got to call in artillery, we don't want them shells landin' on us.

"This all goes on for a couple of hours till we're two or three klicks from the LZ. Smith walks off the trail into the bush a couple of mikes and lays down. 'Time for a rest,' he whispers. Ploughman's all sweaty 'n' tired out. He's tryin' to drink all the water in his canteens at once. 'Slow down on the water,' Smith says. 'You gonna want some of that tomorrow.' It starts to rain 'n' that's good, 'cause noise don't travel when it rains. Another couple of hours, 'n' Smith heads off the trail again. When we hunker down, Smith gets close up to my face 'n' whispers, 'I'm thinkin' we're close, LT. We bin headin' northwest for about four klicks. The trail's gotta be around here somewhere. You want to call in some willy peter so's we kin get a good location?' I get on the horn and radio back to HQ, give them some coordinates, and ask them to shoot two rounds of white phosphorous. We know where they're shooting to and from that we can figure out where we are. Out they come, two rounds, 'n' hit a ways off. 'Not bad,' Smith mutters. 'Jus' a little off.' He marks it on the map.

"Ploughman's having trouble walkin', but he's not complainin'. About 1400 we head off the little trail into the bush. Slow as kin be, we step over branches 'n' stumps, not wantin' to leave any signs. Then it's there, a damn highway of broken rocks 'n' logs, all covered over with triple canopy. We backtrack so's we're far enough away that nobody kin see us, and then we settle down into a little depression behind some fallen logs. There's wet leaves 'n' moldy crap all around us 'n' that's where we set up. Flat, filthy, 'n' part of the terrain, right there in the rain.

The rest of the day goes by all quiet, 'n' the night's pretty much the same. Some kinda animals are crawlin' around us, but they don't get too close. I spend my time watchin' a colony of ants building a little bunker in front of my face. I drop a couple of crumbs from my crackers 'n' watch them swarm, then I put the crackers off to the side 'n' the whole crowd moves over there. Smith's got the first watch, 'n' I'm off to sleep.

In the mornin', I'm up and listenin' for activity on the trail. I got the last watch 'cause we think that the gooks like to move just before dawn. But there's nothin'. I'm eatin' my fruit salad outta the can 'n' wantin' a smoke real bad. Smith's up, 'n' I crawl off a ways 'n' take a piss. As I'm comin' back on my hands and knees, though, I think I hear somethin'. Not from the trail but from behind us, pretty far back but in the bush. I stop 'n' listen. Last thing we need is bad guys bustin' bush right through our position. Sun's out, although it's hard to see through the high cover of the trees; it's already hot; 'n' I'm startin' to sweat. Every nerve in my body is racin'. Very slowly I crawl back to Smith. 'You hear that?' I whisper. Ploughman's still sleepin', 'n' Smith taps him on the shoulder.

"'Ploughman. Ploughman. Wake up. Don't say nothin', 'n' don't move. We got gooks.' Smith is up on his knees and raises his body. Course he can't see nothin' 'cause there's tree's 'n' bushes, shadows, 'n' stumps all around. Frankly, gentlemen, I'm about to shit myself, but there's nothin' to do but wait.

"Next thing that happens is we hear gooks comin' down the trail. Not sure how many, but they're makin' a lot of noise. They sound like they got some kinda wagon, 'n' we can hear the wheels rollin' over the rocks. 'Where's the damn rain when you need it?' Smith whispers. Ploughman rolls over 'n' grabs his 16. He's pointing it at the trail, 'n' when he clicks his safety off, it sounds like a goddamn bell gettin' rung. I'm lookin' out at the trail to see if the gooks heard us 'n' listenin' to the noise comin' from behind us. We see six young girls with big straw hats 'n' black pajamas roll by, pushin' some kind of artillery piece. They're all talkin' at once, gigglin' 'n' such. Then they roll on by and are gone. Smith pulls out a pad from his chest pocket 'n' writes down what we saw. Then he turns around 'n' starts to listen to what's comin' the other way. The noise is gettin' closer 'n' closer. The sound is wide too. Like maybe there's a whole company of 'em bustin' bush to get to the trail. 'N' they're gonna go right through our position. Birds stop chirpin'; now's there's nothin' but them gooks comin' our way. 'Think we gotta move,' I say, so low I'm not sure if anybody hears me. But Smith's gatherin' up his gear and stuffs my empty C rat can in his pocket.

"'We're gonna have to walk on the trail to get outta here, LT. No other way.'

"'Oh, shit,' Ploughman pipes in. 'I ain't goin' on that trail. No way.' He's breathin' real hard, and it looks like he's cryin', although it's hard to tell. His skin's so white, I'm thinkin' he's gonna pass out.

"'Gotta go, Ploughman. No way 'round it.' I grab his poncho liner and start crawling for the trail. We hit it pretty fast 'n' start down the road, makin' all kinds of noise 'cause of the broken rocks. I'm thinkin' maybe it'll be better if we run a bit, at least put some distance between us 'n' them. But Ploughman's hobblin' so bad 'n' breathin' so hard, we're not movin' very fast.

"'Get off the road, LT, they're comin' up on us!' Smith grabs Ploughman's shoulder harness and makes a right turn into the bush on the other side of the road. I turn around 'n' follow them back deep in the trees before we stop, line up our weapons, 'n' get ready to shoot it out.

"Now the noise seems thunderous; I mean, the trees are movin', bushes are shakin'. These guys don't care how much racket they're makin'. I'm thinkin' it's got to be a big outfit to come trampin' through the bush like that. Ploughman's whimperin' now, whisperin', 'Oh, shit… Oh, shit.' Smith's locked 'n' loaded, waitin' for the first one to hit the trail. I get a couple of grenades out and line them up in front of me. My asshole's tighter than a drum, 'n' I don't think I took a breath for at least two minutes.

"Then, the first one comes onto the trail. Smith takes him out with one shot and down he flops. All hell breaks loose. There's screechin' 'n' cryin', the trees are shakin', 'n' a hunnert monkeys gather 'round their little buddy wonderin' what happened. 'Appears we been chased by a battalion o' monkeys,' Smith mutters. 'Well, I'll be goddamned!' Smith's a cool customer, but there's clearly relief in his voice. Now Ploughman's ballin', sobbin' so hard he's makin' a lot of noise. We grab him up 'n' move farther down the road into the woods and settle in. I got to tell ya, I still shake every time I think about it."

Knight lights a cigarette and stands up.

"What happened after that?" Lucifer asks.

Knight smiles. "I called in artillery on their position 'n' blew every one o' them little fuckers away! Since we was compromised; we got outta there that afternoon. Ploughman's now the clerk in the headquarters company, 'n' I'm goin' to Vung fuckin' Tau!"

"Damn," was all Swede said. "Now it's your turn, Cantor...Tell us your fairytale."

CANTOR'S FAIRYTALE:

Cantor was looking grim. He'd had about all the beer he could handle and was chain-smoked out. His mouth tasted like the bottom of an ashtray, and his mind was gray, just gray. He felt the weariness in his muscles, in his lungs, and in his mind. He felt old and sore. He just wanted to get away...far, far away. But everyone was looking at him, and so he took a deep breath and started in.

"There's a guy in my company, a real numb nuts. You know the kind. Can't pack his ruck right, never cleans his weapon, falls asleep on ambush, don't wash...ever. He comes in a few months ago with buck sergeant strips on. Seems he's spent some time in OCS and when they booted him, they give him some rank before they shipped him out. First they give him a squad to run, 'cause he's a sergeant 'n' all, but they catch him one night putting claymores up backward, so when they go off, they blast the guys in the squad when they set 'em off. Fortunately, this all gets caught before he kills anyone, but this guy's dangerous and everybody knows it. It's only a matter of time. The guys get together and go to the first sergeant and complain, tell him they won't go in the bush with him if he's in charge. The first sergeant's pissed at the guys, but he checks it out, talks to the lieutenant and then the company commander. Everybody's watchin' this guy for a week or two, but they can't really discipline him, you know, have him burnin' shit, etc., 'cause he's a sergeant. So they let it go. Give the squad to somebody else and have him trailing along in the back like some kind of dog.

"I talked to this guy a few weeks ago when we were back in the rear. He's all alone in the bunker; everyone else is off at the club, and he's got his arms pretty tight around a bottle of Jack Daniels. He's mumbling something 'bout how he's got to get out of the infantry—can't measure up. You know, scared all the time and depressed. He's looking at ten more months and figures if he fucks up enough somebody will get it together and demote him, get him out of the field, and give him some kinda job he can handle."

Cantor stands up and begins to walk around the hut. He's stumbling some, but mostly he's getting really pissed, and he's close to screaming as he continues.

"Course that don't happen! Next day we go back to the field. The guys are all hungover and strung out, and they're whispering shit in the choppers before we land. There's a couple of snipers at the LZ, so's everybody's unassing the bird and running like a sombitch toward the woods. One guy, Bishop, gets shot in the leg and goes down. Everybody else keeps on runnin' except for old numb nuts. He stops in the middle of the field, dodgin' bullets, grabs up Bishop, and carries him to the cover of the woods. Well, the snipers fade away, the old man gets a medevac to come in, and Bishop heads back to the States to live the rest of his life a happy fucking man. Got the scene now? Numb nuts saved this guy's life...Got him outta that field and into the woods. Bishop goes home and numb nuts don't even get a fucking 'Thank you very much'!"

Cantor's all but screaming now. He's sweating even though the air conditioner is blasting, and he's hunched over as he wanders the hut back and forth. Kind of like he's looking for something, maybe an answer to a question he's asking himself.

"Now everybody's awake and scared. I mean, there's snipers at the LZ and no reason to believe we're not going to see more gooks before the week is out. You know they're out there, just watching and waiting for the right moment. Makes everybody a bit trigger-happy. I'm trying to calm my guys down as we hit the trail, but frankly I'm a little jittery myself. As we're humpin', a booby trap goes off, and one of the guys from second platoon is medivac'd out with a screwed up leg. Then another guy gets hit by a sniper, and off he goes. It's a long fucking day. Everybody's sweating the beer out, and the bugs are biting something fierce. We're humpin' and stoppin' like we always do, but we don't seem to be getting anywhere…one of them days."

Cantor stops at the bar and jumps up on it. He's sitting, dangling his feet, and mumbling to himself. "Sonofabitch!"

"So anyway, we finally stop for the night and set up a company CP. Numb nuts follows his squad out a couple of mikes into the woods for an ambush, and everybody settles down. Nothing much is happening, until all of a sudden there's some firing at the bush site, and radio calls back to the CP. Seems numb nuts stood up in the middle of the night, turned his back on the squad, and started pissing into the woods. Somebody thought he was a gook and wasted him. They medivac'd him out, but there wasn't much left to save. So's he's seriously dead."

Cantor starts kicking the bar with his feet, seems to get a hold of himself, and jumps down.

"Of course, the next morning we ruck up and continue the hump. All and all it's a pretty average week, and we even get choppers back to the base. Yesterday we had a service for the guys who got medivac'd. You know, chaplain says a prayer; we got a pair of boots, a 16 with a bayonet, and helmet set up. Company commander puts a Bronze Star on the helmet.

"'Sergeant Nun wasn't the best soldier we had in the unit,' the old man says, talking kind of low and embarrassed, 'but he took Specialist Bishop outta that LZ like a real hero. We're gonna miss him.' And then we ate some steaks and got drunk.

"So, Knight." He's looking right at the lieutenant. "That's the story of Sergeant Charlie Nun. What'd you say? 'Nun of this, 'n' nun of that, thank you very much. Couldn't shine his boots in Officer Candidate School'? Fuck you, Lieutenant, and the horse you rode in on!" Cantor sits down and all but passes out in his chair.

"Well, I'll be goddamned," Knight mutters.

"Shit," Swede says, looking at the ceiling. Lucifer doesn't say a thing, just looks embarrassed and kind of confused.

After about ten minutes of nobody saying anything, Swede's snoring, Knight is pissing out the back door of the hut, Cantor's passed out on the table, and Lucifer's just staring at the "BIG RED ONE" poster; the door opens. With a blast of light, in comes the first sergeant, who adjusts his eyes to the dark and looks around the hut kind of disgusted. "Well, men, looks like you already had your party. Clean this shit up, 'cause you're going back to the field. Thunder 111 got hit this morning 'n' all passes are canceled." He looks at Lucifer. "Wake that sombitch up and get a move on. War's back in town!" And out he goes.

Lucifer wakes Cantor and Swede up. Knight continues out the back door. The rest of them police up the beer cans and ashtrays, grab their boonie hats, and stumble out into the sunlight. "Take it slow, pilgrims," Swede mumbles, kind of imitating John Wayne, and sort of laughs. "Don't mean nothin'."

And they all staggered home.

JUSTICE

Everybody said it couldn't be done. I mean, there were never any court-martial trials in the battalion. If somebody fucked up, they just give him extra duty, like burnin' shit for a month or so when he was in the rear. Filling sandbags in the sun after ambushing all night was another one. Stuff like that would get your attention for sure and keep you in line. If you were really bad, I mean, if you hit an officer or got too heavy into the black power thing, you might get transferred up-country to the Americal Division or somethin'. But a trial? The possibility of getting convicted, having a federal conviction on your record, and spending time in a CONEX container at Long Binh jail? Shit like that just didn't happen, 'n' everybody knew it. Like spending a year in the bush wasn't enough?

And the rules about getting to the rear were funny too. I mean, if you were a squad leader and did a real good job, and the first sergeant really liked you, you might find a job back in the rear in a supply room for a couple of months afore you went back to the world. Or if you got the jitters so's everybody began to notice, and you weren't a slacker, just unreliable in the woods, well then, they might take you outta there so's nobody got hurt. Or if you got shot up. That's what happened to me. Ten months in 'n' a grenade went off as we was unloadin' ammo from a chopper, 'n' I got my arm screwed up. They let me work in the battalion mess hall, cleanin' up the tables 'n' moppin' everythin' down. KP sucks but it beats gettin' rained on 'n' playin' shoot 'em up with the little people. Mostly, though, you stayed in the woods right up till the end. Then you came in one night, got a haircut, found your duffel bag in supply, located yourself a pair of khakis, 'n' then got on the freedom bird. The rules weren't written down and for sure they were arbitrary, but everybody kinda knew what they were 'n' accepted them. So's when Singleton came up on charges for stealin' a jeep, everybody was shocked 'n' followed the trial real close. 'Cause if they could get Singleton, they could get anybody.

It wasn't like Singleton was a bad guy either. I mean he was a black sergeant E-5, for sure, but he didn't wear no afro, and wasn't sleepin' with the other black power guys in that special bunker of theirs; he wasn't much for black power salutes or dappin'. And he never carried one of them canes with the knife built into its head. He'd worked as a team leader and then a squad leader with Charlie Company for nine months, got shot once, 'n' they give him a medal for pulling a guy out of a firefight so's he wouldn't get wounded a second time. If he said somethin', it was true. I mean, you could count on Singleton. Mostly, though, he just kept to hisself, did his job, and waited to go home. Which is why they gave him the job of drivin' the battalion executive officer around in his jeep, keepin' the jeep clean 'n' turnin' it in every night to the motor pool for maintenance 'n' such…So's in a way, none o' this made much sense.

Course he did steal the jeep, but even that was complicated. Around that time there was a lot of jeeps for the takin'. The Ninth Infantry had gone home, the Eighty-Second Airborne had gone home, 'n' parts of lots of other units were headin' out. We'd been in Vietnam so long, nobody really knew who owned the equipment they'd brought with them, 'n' with everybody just lookin' to didi out o' there, there was a lot of equipment just layin' around: trucks, gas masks, field tents, wrench kits, water trailers, 'n', of course, jeeps. Mostly if you came in with some item like that, the warrant officers who were in charge of keepin' all this shit straight would just paint over the serial number and put a new one on it. Nobody seemed to mind, 'n' since we was still in the bush and had real work to do…the rear area rules just didn't seem to apply. But things were tightenin' up for sure as it looked like we was gettin' ready to leave too. 'N' salutin', guard mounts, polishin' shit…all that was comin' back into fashion, so's you had to be careful.

'Cause of some new rules that come down, Singleton had a real lawyer workin' for him, but there wasn't no judge or jury. Only three lieutenants from the different companies, who were in the rear 'cause they was executive officers. There was First Lieutenant Craig, who was a West Pointer and lookin' to make the army his career; First Lieutenant Kit, who was an ROTC guy and probably gonna get out; and then there was First Lieutenant Ricky Shane, who was from Officer Candidate School. There was the adjutant, Captain McWilliams, who was assigned to be the prosecutor. They made Specialist Marvin James the court reporter 'cause he was a real lawyer who got drafted and, I suppose, he knew somethin' about the way things was supposed to be run. Of course, all us enlisted guys was rootin' for Singleton. There was a lot of bettin' goin' on as well, 'n' we figured we had a chance with at least Ricky, 'cause he had been through basic like we had and knew somethin' about being a troop.

"Singleton's goin' down," a lot of people thought. "He's black, and even more important than that, the chief don't like him; he refused to change the serial numbers when he brought the jeep into the motor pool. He just turned Singleton in."

'N' that was seriously so. Chief Warrant Officer Johnnie Rivers was a tired old bastard from someplace so far down South even the army never went there. His whole motor pool was white 'n' Dixie 'n' all the black guys knew they had to have their shit together real tight when they turned somethin' in or it was gonna' get rejected for sure. We were pretty sure the chief had looked the other way when serial numbers were changed in the past, but nobody could find anybody who'd admit to it, 'n' that whole crowd at the motor pool wasn't sayin' nothin'.

So's the day came when the trial was to begin. Ricky, Lieutenant Craig, 'n' Lieutenant Kit set up a table in the mess hall right after chow and commenced to drinkin' coffee 'n' smokin' cigarettes. Marvin James comes in 'n' asks me for three more tables, one for the prosecution, one for the defense, 'n' one for him to sit at and take notes. Since I'm the mess orderly, I help them get their stuff together and then go about cleanin' up. Nobody notices me 'cause I'm invisible...So's I got to see the whole thing. The fans are buzzin', the flies are all over the place like they always are right after chow, 'n' it's seriously hot. Jus' another day in the Nam—nothin' special.

In comes Singleton and his defense counsel, a short little guy with glasses who is a captain but looks to be about twelve years old. He's as clean as can be 'n' lookin' kind of uncomfortable, like maybe it's the first time he's come visiting us grunts, down here along the perimeter.

"Morning gentlemen," this captain says. All the lieutenants stand up, but James stays at his desk shuffling his pad like he's got something important to do. Really, he just don't want to stand up for no military lawyer. Singleton's quiet, all cleaned up, but sweatin' 'n' nervous. He knows he's guilty. The green machine has finally got him in its clutches 'n' he's just waitin' to see how bad it's gonna be. I'm washin' chairs down, but nobody gives a shit.

Lieutenant Craig shakes hands with the captain and says "Morning. This here's Lieutenant Kit and Lieutenant Shane. Guess we're the jury today." He looks at Kit. "I suppose I got time and grade, so I'm the board president." Nobody says hello to Singleton, and they all sit down. After McWilliams comes in, he nods to everybody and commences to shufflin' some papers.

"You got the script?" he asks James.

"Right here, sir," James says, looking all efficient. "Got the charge sheet, the orders for the court, the list of witnesses, and the Bible to swear people in. Got a copy of the Uniform Code of Military Justice too, case you want to consult it." He drops it all on McWilliams desk with a loud thud. It's clear he don't think a military court can do much justice without a judge, a proper jury, more lawyers, 'n' maybe a court-room that don't look like it just finished servin' up eggs 'n' sos to a bunch of grunts. Then he commences to pass out copies of everything to everybody 'cept Singleton, 'n' they get to reading. After a while, McWilliams looks up at Craig 'n' says, "You ready?" 'N' off they go.

The beginning of a trial apparently requires a lot of reading things out loud. McWilliams reads the order signed by the brigade command-er who convened the court. McWilliams swears in the board, and they swear him in; then he reads the charge sheet, which of course every-body's got in front of them.

"Article 121, Larceny and Wrongful Appropriation:

(a) Any person subject to this chapter who wrongfully takes, ob-tains, or withholds, by any means, from the possession of the owner or of any other person any money, personal property, or article of value of any kind—
(1) With intent permanently to deprive or defraud another per-son of the use of and benefit of property or to appropriate it to his own use or the use of any other person other than the owner, steals that property and is guilty of larceny; or
(2) With intent to temporarily deprive or defraud another per-son of the use and benefit of property, or to appropriate it to his own use or the use of any person other than the owner, is guilty of wrongful appropriation.
(b) Any person found guilty of larceny or wrongful appropriation shall be punished as a court-martial may direct."

After that, McWilliams looks around and asks me for a cup of cof-fee, which I get him, and he outlines what happens if Singleton is found guilty. He can go to jail for six months, which means he stays in the

Nam six months longer than his year. He can lose some money and get busted down to private as well. It's a federal conviction that follows you for the rest of your life. Except for the fans, the place is real quiet, like everybody realizes for the first time that this shit's for real, and somebody could get hurt.

Craig reads from his script. "Sergeant Singleton, do you understand the charge that has been filed against you?" Singleton stands up with his defense counsel and says that he does. "So, how do you plead?"

'N' now the captain says, "My client pleads to the charge and specification 'not guilty,' sir." He says "sir" even though Craig is only a lieutenant, and the little captain outranks him. Guess you want to be nice to one of the guys who's gonna decide what happens to your client. Makes sense.

Craig looks over at James, who says real quiet, "Opening statements."

"Captain McWilliams, proceed with your opening statement." McWilliams got some notes, but it don't look like he really needs 'em. Everybody in the battalion knows what happened. He describes how Singleton was the duty driver for the battalion XO, Major Ambrosino, who directed him to take him to Saigon one afternoon to visit a friend. That's where I almost lost it. Ambrosino was visiting a whorehouse, like he always does on Tuesday afternoons when the battalion commander is in the field with the companies. Sometimes he would let the clerk go with him, but he never let Singleton inside 'cause he was supposed to be guarding the jeep. McWilliams continues, even as everybody else but Singleton 'n' the little captain are smirkin' 'n' smilin' at each other.

"When Major Ambrosino returned to the street," McWilliams continues, "Sergeant Singleton picked him up in a jeep other than the one he had used to transport the major. Seems somebody stole Singleton's jeep. They returned to base before dark, and Sergeant Singleton dropped the major off at the battalion headquarters. Thereafter, he apparently cleaned the vehicle and attempted to turn it in to Chief Rivers at the motor pool. Rivers discovered the vehicle was not the one signed out to Singleton in the morning and reported Singleton to battalion

for failing to secure his vehicle and for stealing someone else's vehicle."
McWilliams stops and looks at Craig. "Appears to be a cut 'n' dry case.
We will call Warrant Officer Rivers to testify to these facts." He sits
down, 'n' before Craig can say anything else, the little captain stands up
'n' says he is going to waive his opening statement.

Craig looks at James. "We got time for a cigarette break before
the chief comes in?" James nods, and Craig mumbles about being ad-
journed and goes outside for a butt.

Now it's rainin', 'n' the three lieutenants are standing under the eve
of the Quonset hut smokin'. Nobody's sayin' anything. They're just
staring out at the rain, each thinkin', I suppose, how lucky they are to
be inside 'n' not sleepin' out in the mud. Chief Rivers comes walkin' by
and gives the lieutenants one of them "I don't really have to salute you
'cause you only lieutenants 'n' I'm a chief" salutes and walks inside. He's
talkin' to McWiliams as the others come back in, and then Craig says as
he's sittin' down, "This court is called to order. Captain McWilliams,
please call your witness."

McWilliams calls Rivers to the stand and has him swear to tell the
truth, the whole truth, 'n' all that. He shows him the property book,
and Rivers talks about how it proves Singleton signed out a jeep with a
particular serial number and never returned it. It's an army vehicle 'n'
costs the government a couple of grand. 'N' now it's gone. "So Chief,"
McWilliams says, standin' up 'n' lookin' at the lieutenants, "is there
any doubt in your mind that Sergeant Singleton stole the vehicle he
attempted to turn into you…That it wasn't the vehicle he signed out of
the motor pool that morning?"

The little captain stands up 'n' near yells over the rain hitting the tin
roof of the hut. "I object, Mr. President. Facts not in evidence. Surely
the chief here has no way of knowing what was on Sergeant Singleton's
mind when he returned the jeep. Calls for speculation." Everybody's
shocked, since the little captain hasn't said very much before, 'n' nobody was expecting much from him. Craig looks a bit confused, 'n' he
looks over at James, who is smiling and nodding his head.

"Well, I suppose you're right there, Captain. The witness will not answer the question. Anything else, Captain McWilliams?" McWilliams looks pissed, like he's going to give Craig what for once the trial is over and it's back to him being a lieutenant 'n' McWilliams outranking him.

"OK," McWilliams says to the chief. "What was the serial number on the vehicle that left the motor pool with Singleton in the morning, and what was the serial number when it was returned?"

The chief looks at his property book. "They was different," he says. "The one that left had a number 583412, 'n' the one that come back was 345213." McWilliams smiles and kind of scowls at the little captain.

"That will be all, chief." 'N' McWilliams sits down.

Now the little captain gets up 'n' stands next to the lieutenants' table. "What did you do with the vehicle 345213? The one Sergeant Singleton returned to your care, custody and control?"

The chief's face blanches white right through his tan, 'n' he looks at McWilliams, who fairly bleats out, "I object. What happened to the second vehicle has nothing to do with the question of whether Singleton stole it." Craig looks over at James, who kind of shrugs like "This one's on you, lieutenant." Kit reaches over 'n' whispers something in Craig's ear, 'n' they go back 'n' forth for a minute. Ricky ain't sayin' nothin'.

"I think I want to hear the answer to that question," says Craig.

"Well, sir, the motor pool initiated an investigation pursuant to regulation and determined that the vehicle was not on our property books. Then we took appropriate action."

"An investigation, yes. Did you make an inquiry as to what unit had the vehicle on its property book?" The little captain is lookin' at his notes.

"Well, no. Because we are involved in combat operations, we are not required to do that." The chief's still white as rice but hopin' the little captain don't know nothin' about motor pool regulations.

"So where is the vehicle now?" The little captain looks up and nods at Craig.

"In my motor pool," says the chief.

"And what did you do with it there?" the little captain asks, like he don't know the answer.

Chief sees he don't have a way out and mumbles, "We changed the serial number and officially registered it as equipment of the battalion as per army regulation."

"Just so we're clear," says the little captain. "According to you, Sergeant Singleton signed out a jeep owned by the United States Army at the direction of the battalion XO, a vehicle that was on the books of the battalion. He drove the vehicle. He returned a jeep owned by the United States Army that is presently on the books of the battalion, a vehicle that presently has the same serial number as the one Sergeant Singleton signed out. Is that correct?" The little captain's starin' at the chief, 'n' he ain't impressed.

"Well, if you put it that way," says the chief, all deflated, "that is correct." 'N' of course there ain't no further questions.

Captain McWilliams don't have anything else. The property book is admitted into evidence, and then he rests. The little captain says he don't have nothin' to present except Singleton's personnel record, 'n' he rests too. After that, everybody shuffles their papers, 'n' the little captain makes a closing statement about how Singleton is a good non-commissioned officer 'n' never did nothin' but support the battalion during his time here in Vietnam, the Republic of. He says there's no proof that Singleton ever used the jeep for anything other than US Army business, so's how can they call it larceny? Finally, he says what a damn shame it would be to ruin a man's life over all of this. He speaks pretty good, 'n' later we all agree it was probably good for the army to give Singleton a lawyer to represent him.

McWilliams talks for a long time but don't say much. He does point out that "even good troops can do bad things" and goes on about what would happen if everybody was allowed to break regulations 'n' steal shit whenever they wanted. "Sergeant Singleton is a noncommissioned officer," McWilliams says at the end, "'n' should of known better. This ain't the Wild West."

After that, everybody leaves the mess hall 'cept the lieutenants, who get some more coffee 'n' commence to talkin' it all out. I got nothin' else to do, but I decide to wash the windows so's I kin hear what they're sayin'. There's a bunch 'o guys standin' outside in the rain waitin' but nobody from the motor pool, which makes sense 'cause them bastards caused all this shit in the first place. "It's only a fuckin' jeep," Kit starts out. "What the fuck!" Seems he's pissed. "Why we gotta convict a guy of stealin' a jeep, when he brought it back and the only reason he's in trouble is 'cause the chief don't like him?"

"Well, I can't say I disagree with you. But I'm looking at the charge sheet here, and he's definitely guilty of misappropriation, if not larceny. Guess we got to follow the law. We took an oath." Craig looks defeated. He wants to let Singleton go but don't see a way out. "Where you at on this, Shane?" 'N' that's when my jaw dropped.

Ricky lights a cigarette, exhales, 'n' looks at the two of them. "Man stole a jeep. It wasn't his to take, and he failed to secure the vehicle he was supposed to protect. Singleton's a good kid, but he's an NCO and should have known better. We're officers; we took an oath to follow the law. So I got to vote guilty. Don't mean we have to send him to the stockade though." 'N' there it was. The green machine's rules and regulation versus some kinda' understanding of what was really goin' on.

"You know the only reason the chief is doin' this is 'cause Singleton is black," says Craig.

"Yeah maybe, but we can't take that into consideration. The rules are pretty clear. Man can't steal somethin' just because somebody else stole his vehicle first. Otherwise, I'm thinkin' I like that nice shiny bowie knife you're wearin'. Mebbe when you're not lookin' I just take it off you 'n' call it mine. Got to follow the rules, or there's nothin' but a gaggle of men doin' whatever they want. That ain't no army." Ricky's adamant. I'm thinkin' he's makin' sense, even if I don't like what he's sayin'.

"You suppose there's times when, assuming the right facts, a jury can ignore the strict letter of the law and let somebody go for other reasons?" Craig is reading and reading the charge sheet.

"Chief did put the jeep back on the books. US Army never lost the vehicle after all. Does that make a difference?" Kit goes for another cup of coffee. Walks right past me without saying a word.

"I don't see how." Ricky knows there're rules 'n' then theys "rules" in the army. Nothin' operates by the book. Some guys salute; other guys don't. Some guys shoot a gook when they shouldn't, 'n' they let it slide. Fog of battle 'n' all that. Nobody's even sure why we in this fuckin' war anymore. Everybody's just waitin' to go home...even the officers. "Not sure this thing should have gotten to the level of a court-martial, but here we are. If we don't follow the rules, who's gonna? What happens to the guys who do follow the rules? What's," he sighs, "the fuckin' point?"

"Yeah, I get that...but still." Kit looks like he's ready to cry. "Don't seem right."

Craig's reading the charge sheet again. "Battalion commander is going to be pissed," he mumbles under his breath. "Real pissed. We got to be unanimous, whatever we do." 'N' I'm thinkin', "Here we go. Fuckin' lifers lookin' out for their careers again."

"Fuck it," Kit all but screams. "I am not convicting Sergeant Singleton for losing a jeep in front of a whorehouse so the battalion XO can get his rocks off, and the chief can stick it to another black kid. Not sure I give a shit what the law says."

Craig says, "Let's read the charge sheet one more time and then vote. Whatever we decide, its got to be unanimous and we keep it to ourselves. Agreed?" Everybody nods and then sets to reading. I'm about shitting in my pants 'cause I'm thinkin' Singleton is fucked, 'n' I got twenty bucks on his beatin' this thing.

When it's all said and done, though, they find Singleton not guilty and announce it in open court. They're all lookin' a bit sheepish 'n' real unhappy. But everybody outside is hootin' 'n' hollerin, 'n' even McWilliams seems kinda relieved. The little captain thanks the lieutenants and shakes Singleton's hand. Singleton don't smile, but he does shake the lieutenants' hands before he goes out the back door. He 'n' the crowd all go the EM club to get drunk, which I can't do 'cause I got to help get the next meal together. But I gotta say, that smile didn't come off my face for three days. Rumor was the lieutenants all got a talkin' to by the battalion commander, but not too much. Seems he was happy they let Singleton go even if he wasn't sure the lieutenants really followed their oath 'n' acted like good officers.

Things got tougher at the motor pool, and there was a lot of "nigger" this and "nigger" that goin' around. But one night somebody caught Rivers when he was stumblin' outta the officers' club, and put a hurt on him. Everythin' sorta calmed down after that, and eventually most of us got to go home alive.

O TEMPORA, O MORES![1]
–CICERO

When Aloysius Toole hit Officer Candidate School at Fort Benning, Georgia in the spring of 1968, he had dropped out of college and didn't have a clue what he was going to do with the rest of his life. He didn't really want to be an officer, and certainly not an infantry officer, especially after all the crap he had taken in basic and the follow-on infantry training. Being a draftee, he was headed to Vietnam, for sure, which was all right with him. It was, in a sense, just one more thing. He wasn't in charge of his life anymore and had gotten kind of used to just letting things slide. "Don't mean nuthin'," the black guys in the barracks used to say. "Don't mean a goddamn thing!" Toole figured they had it about right. And like a spectator, he waited to see what the next big thing in his life would be. He didn't have to wait long.

His father had died the year before. Inexplicably disappeared from his life. He lost his biggest fan when it happened—nobody left to really root for him when he put on pads and played running back at Youngstown College, and it bit hard. One night, just before his junior year, he got drunk and hit an assistant coach who was giving him a

---

1 Cicero: *"Oh the times! Oh the customs!"*

good deal of grief about how he was playing. He had to admit, it felt pretty good slapping that graduate student around. But then, of course, he was off the team and back to being just a student. Toole never was much of a learner, and so he let it all go. First math, then philosophy, and finally even history went by the wayside. No classes attended and no passing grades received. He didn't even bother to show up for his finals. Just slid on out the door and waited for the draft to pick him up. And in 1967, it didn't take long.

Toole figured he'd take his training, go to Vietnam and then get out—maybe get an early out—and go back to school. But it didn't work out that way. First they sent him to Fort Campbell, Kentucky, where he was part of a new unit, the Sixth Infantry Division, filling in for the 101st Airborne Division that was going to Vietnam. The place was crazy with being 101st; everybody else on the post was just an interloper or a coward. At the enlisted club, the guys from the division would get real drunk and then find somebody in the Sixth to beat up. You had to have friends and stick with them, or it could mean a beating for sure. And Toole was a loner. It wasn't that he was smarter than anybody else or that he had been to college. In the army, that sort of thing didn't matter. His bunkmate was a teacher, and his squad mates were either high school dropouts or guys like him who had blown their 2S deferments. Everybody had a story, but at the end of the day it was all about how well you could run, and shine your shoes, and fire your weapon. If you were a draftee, the point was to stay out of everyone's hair, stay way below the radar, and hope nobody noticed you. It was all a lottery of sorts, like the list that came down every first day of the month with guys' names who were called out of the Sixth and sent to the war. One day you were a number in the first sergeant's roster list, called to do KP or some other shit detail, and the next you had two weeks leave and you were gone. Being a loner kept you out of trouble, but still the list happened, and you were on it or off it for another month depending on nothing more than chance. Sometimes it got very old letting chance decide what was going to happen, and Toole gave that some thought. He had choices, his mind would argue. He could go to the EM Club alone, get drunk, and let the 101st guys beat the shit out of him. He could skip the club and hit the movies. But they ended at nine o'clock, and then he would still have the rest of the weekend to kill. Or he could get some friends for protection. He had choices, sure, but none of them were good.

One afternoon at 1600, a sergeant he didn't really know gathered him up as he was walking back to the barracks from a cleaning detail at battalion. "Toole. You Private Toole?" the sergeant asked. He was an E7; that is, a platoon sergeant, and therefore kind of important. Toole stopped in his tracks and looked around.

"Yes, Sergeant, that's me." He hadn't been out of basic that long and was still wary of senior people talking to him. "Keep your mouth shut, maybe they'll go away," he thought. He knew by now that sergeants couldn't hit you or even harass you much anymore, but they still had the ear of the first sergeant. You could find yourself on the wrong end of a million details if you pissed them off. They might even have something to do with that war list.

"Lieutenant wants to talk to you. He'll be in the dayroom at 1700 hours. You be there too, all nice and clean. Got it?" The sergeant waited for an answer, but it was clear he wasn't going to wait too long.

"What's that about?" Toole asked. "I haven't done anything wrong." Officers never talked to privates, at least not in the infantry stateside. Like the first sergeant said when he addressed the formation the first day at Fort Campbell: "The captain here is your daddy and I'm your mommy. We ain't married see, so's you know what that makes you! Believe me, you don't never want to meet the captain by hisself. He only got medals or court-martials on his mind. 'N' there ain't no medals here at Fort Campbell."

"Beats the shit out of me," replied the older man. "Mebbe he wants to make you his bitch. An aid or somethin'." The platoon sergeant laughed at his own joke. "You be there, boy, or the First Shirt's gonna hear about it!" he said over his shoulder as he walked away. "Jus' be there."

Toole picked up his step. "What would an officer want with me?" he asked himself. "How's he even know my name?" Toole got to the barracks and went to his locker. He pulled out a clean set of fatigues and cursed. He didn't want to iron another pair for the next day and definitely didn't want to sit up all night and spit shine his boots. But you had to look good for an officer, and even if the first sergeant wasn't going to be there, he'd hear about it. "Got to look good," he thought. At 1450 he was standing in front of the dayroom door. He wanted to go outside and smoke a cigarette, but he was afraid he might be late, or that the officer might come out early, or that something else might happen. Better to stay there and be early. "Do what you're told," he thought, "and they'll leave you alone."

At 1505, the door opened and a little guy with reddish hair, starched fatigues, and glasses looked at him. He had a clipboard in his hand. Toole read him. He had no combat infantryman's badge, no jump wings, and no combat patch. He wore adjutant general's brass, and his hair was pretty long. This guy was clearly some ROTC puke doing his two years, just like Toole, but he had probably graduated from college and was definitely getting paid better. "Private Toole, come on in." He smiled and turned around. "You go by Aloysius, or do you have another name?" He walked to a field desk next to the green Ping-Pong table in the middle of the room and sat down. He waved his right hand for Toole to sit down.

"Back home they called me Tony," Toole said as he sat. "In the army, I'm just Toole." And then he waited. The lieutenant had a stack of folders on the table—personnel records like Toole had hand-carried from Fort Dix to Fort Campbell months ago.

"Toole, I've been looking over your records. Impressive. Some college, football player. You were an Eagle Scout when you were younger, weren't you?"

Toole woke up and started to listen. "There's no way this guy should know that much about me. This can't be good," he thought.

"Yes sir," Toole responded.

"What was your major?" the lieutenant asked. He was checking boxes off some form in the file.

"Well, I was a history major. Kind of liked literature as well." Toole was wary. He hadn't even had this conversation with his bunk mate, the teacher.

"I was poli sci at Dartmouth...Why'd you quit?" The redhead looked up and over his glasses at Toole, who was beginning to wonder if the army was going to punish him for quitting college. He really didn't know why he had quit. It was just something that had happened after his father died, like giving his car away to his little brother and getting his draft notice. One day you're painting houses and living at home, reading books and waiting for the mail. And the next, your friends and neighbors get a hold of you and you're on a bus to Fort Dix.

"Sir, I don't really know." Toole looked around the dayroom, noticed the 101st "Screaming Eagles" signs on the walls, the ashtrays, and the magazines. The dayroom was a place where you were supposed to be able to go after a long day in the field and relax. They gave you some reading material and a Ping-Pong table. There was a coffee machine in the corner, but there was never any coffee to make. It had been taken over by the black guys in the unit, their private clubhouse. So a white guy with a busted 2S deferment wasn't really welcome. He'd been there once, to see if he could get a magazine to read up on the news on his way to guard mount. The first sergeant had a thing about the news. Wanted his privates to know what was going on. So if you had to go to guard mount, you would report to him first with your weapon. He would check your uniform, inspect your weapon, and ask you questions about what was in *Time* magazine. "Soldier's got to know why he fightin'," he would say. He would ask you your general orders and something about the Code of Conduct, and you would answer him from memory. "I am an American fighting man. I serve in the forces that guard my country and its way of life. I am prepared to die in their defense."

"Who's the president, Toole?"

"President Johnson, First Sergeant."

"Why we fightin' in Vietnam?" Well, of course, that was the $64,000 question. There were a million answers to that one, but Toole had always found that none of them were particularly satisfying. Maybe it was to help the Vietnamese stay out of the clutches of the communists from the North; maybe it was to keep the Russians and the Chinese from taking over the world. Maybe it was about keeping the big industries flush with jobs and profits. Some thought it had something to do with boredom. The politicians had this big old army and nothing to do with it. Every so often you had to have a war just to keep everybody trained up and ready. One guy, a black fellow from Detroit, was certain it was a racial conspiracy. "This war's about keeping the brothers down," he would announce. "Draft all the brothers, jus' to keep 'em in line, 'n' let 'em know who's boss!" With all the riots going on around the country, Toole thought that one made some sense. But, of course, he wasn't going to say that out loud.

"Well, from my perspective, First Sergeant, I'm going to be fighting in Vietnam because I am ordered to do it." The First Shirt always liked that answer. "You gonna be all right, Toole. Jus' keep doin' what you're doin'. Let the politicians figure out the big stuff. Now you get on off to guard mount and make the company proud. We're dependin' on you."

Toole's mind bounced back to the lieutenant. "After my father died, I thought I would do my two years and then go back to school on the GI Bill. He would have understood that." Toole's dad had been in World War II and always prided himself on serving his country—a rite of passage, like getting your driver's license and signing up for the draft, or earning your first paycheck. "Sometimes a man's got to step up when the country calls," he would say. The officer seemed satisfied with that answer. He checked off another box.

"Well, the army's got something else in mind for you. We want to send guys like you, experienced guys with good test scores, to Officer Candidate's School at Fort Benning, and earn you a commission. Make your dad proud. What do you think about that?" He looked directly at Toole to measure his answer. Toole was confused. The idea that he could be an officer had never entered his mind. It wasn't that they were any smarter than him. Hell, they were just guys in his class who had finished up college instead of dropping out. Some of them seemed to know what they were doing, but there were a lot of them bumbling around like he was. They always dressed up well, though, and had starched fatigues from the dry cleaners and really shined boots. They had great cars and seemed to be enjoying what they were doing; no KP or shit details for them. And he assumed they always had some money in their pockets. He remembered envying them when he was out in the woods patrolling. The lieutenant was always up front with a map. When he would stop to figure out where they were, Toole would always have to get down in the mud and look out to his left or right. Even if the lieutenant just wanted to stop and scratch his ass, the soldiers would have to get into the mud, which after the fifth or sixth time got very old. It was cold down there and wet. There were days when he wanted to be up front, scratching his ass and staying out of the mud. Days when he could stay clean and dry, and tell the sergeants where to go and what to do. Days when he would actually have something to say about who he was and where he was going.

Toole knew his answer could make a difference. If he sounded like a wise-ass, he could piss the lieutenant off. The first sergeant would surely hear about it, and Toole would wind up on some really shitty details—KP every other day, for example. Or worse, the army would write him off as a troublemaker. He could wind up on that war list and be gone. He was way above the radar now, and the electric noise in his ears was deafening.

"Well, sir," Toole started his answer slowly. "Being an officer would surely be important. But I'm not looking to make the army a career or anything. I just sort of assumed I would do my two-year obligation and get out." He tried to look the lieutenant in the eyes to show him that he was sincere and not trying to buck the system. "Never really gave it much thought...."

The lieutenant looked like he had heard that answer before, and Toole was relieved to see that he didn't seem pissed off. "Toole, you got a chance here. Most of us aren't going to stay in the army after our time is done. But while we're here, we're going to take the opportunity to contribute what we can. You've got what it takes to be an officer. It would be a shame to waste this chance to make something of yourself." He waited. "And the commitment's not that much longer—just another ten months." Toole did the private's calculation in his head. He knew, like every soldier, what his ETS was—estimated time of separation. He'd done eight months already so he only had sixteen months to go. But if he went to OCS, he would add another year or so onto his commitment. He would be twenty-three when he got out rather than twenty-two. On the other hand, he wouldn't have to do KP anymore, get beat up at the EM club, and spend all those long waking hours in his bunk waiting for the loneliness to stop. He wouldn't be broke anymore, borrowing money from other busted privates to get a pack of cigarettes or go to the movies. He wouldn't be waiting, always waiting, for the dull pain to stop. And furthermore, he wouldn't be checking every month for the list to grab him up and send him off.

"Sir, this is certainly an opportunity. Maybe I should think on it awhile." He wanted to get out of the dayroom fast, before the lieutenant made him sign something. He knew not to sign anything if he could help it. The army had taught him that. In basic, the sergeant had put a form in front of him and told him to sign. That little exercise had cost him precious money out of his pay, because he was now the owner of a fifty-dollar US savings bond and a contributor to some charity for soldiers. The officer seemed encouraged.

"Well, Toole, you seem interested. Tomorrow I'm going to set up an appointment with your company commander, and we'll talk some more. Believe me," he said, "getting a commission will be the best thing that ever happened to you." Toole stood up, said "Thank you, sir," did a fairly crisp about-face and walked out the door. When he hit the hallway, he muttered, "What the fuck?" and went to his bunk. Later, he changed into his civilian clothes and went to the EM club, got very drunk, and pondered his future.

The entire base was buzzing that evening. The guys from the 101st were still in their new jungle fatigues and drinking like the beer taps were going to stop pouring. They had been waiting in long lines all day for busses to take them to the airport. They were sitting on their duffel bags, with their weapons and web gear and all their other equipment, catcalling the soldiers who were not going on the busses. "Heh, pussy," they were screaming at anyone who would listen to them. But, of course, they were being ignored by everyone, and that just pissed them off more. "Why ain't you goin' to Vietnam? Come on over here, you leg mothafucka! I'll show you 'bout bein' a soldier, Airbone!" Toole had averted his eyes and kept on walking as he made it to the club. When they closed the place down, the 101st guys went back to their duffel bag lines and slept there waiting for the busses through the night. Toole could hear them as he lay in his bunk, screaming up at the barracks windows. The noise was deafening. Guys were yelling at each other and fighting, throwing rocks at the windows, and carrying on. As it got closer to midnight, the rocks stopped, but there were still some drunk guys lying out in the field under the windows, close to passing out. "I don' want ta go to Vietnam! I don't want to die in some rice paddy over dere." Some guys were crying and others just moaning—all the bravado gone, all the violence beat out of them. They were puking on the grass and lying in the dirt. "Oh, momma, get me outta this shit. I gotta get outta this shit!" Nobody in the barracks said much; even the soul brothers had turned down their boom boxes and gave the night away to the crying troops.

It was a long night, and Toole had stayed awake for most of it. In the morning, though, the 101st guys were all gone, disappeared as if they had never been there in the first place. Toole got up when the corporal came 'round and took a shower. Everybody in the barracks was quiet, like they were embarrassed for the 101st guys. Like they'd been to a funeral and there was nothing more to say. They got up, put on their fatigues, and went to formation. Just another day in the big green machine.

When Toole hit the dayroom at 1700 hours, he was scared to death. The first sergeant had told him that the company commander was going to be in there, and Toole didn't want to see him. He didn't want the company commander to know his name, and he definitely didn't want the company commander to think Toole wasn't respectful of what the army was offering. "This can't end well," he thought as he waited, adjusting and readjusting his gig line so the buttons on his shirt lined up with his belt buckle and his fly. He stared at the pictures on the wall. The first sergeant and company commander were represented, then the battalion commander, the division commander, and the secretary of defense. Finally, the president had his picture too. The entire chain of command. Toole knew he was the little speck of dust at the far right corner, the interchangeable private—no picture, no name tag. Not a mention, and he liked it that way. But now the bright light was on him. Whatever he decided, the company commander would know him and be able to pick him out from the crowd. And that couldn't be good.

At lunch, he had called his mother and told her what the army wanted to do with him. "Well, Tony," she had said, "you've got to do what you feel is right. It would be nice to have an officer in the family. Your dad would be real proud, but I just don't know." She paused. "Could you still get home every now and then and see us?" They had left it at that. He told her he would think about it and let her know. Clearly, he was on his own. So when the door opened and the lieutenant greeted him with, "Come on in, Tony," Toole still didn't know what to do.

The captain was seated behind the table, drinking coffee from a mug with a 101st Screaming Eagle on the side. He was looking down at a file and told him to sit down. He was older than most captains, with some gray hair and a short graying moustache. He wore fatigues with all sorts of badges—the combat infantryman's badge, jump wings, a ranger tab, and a combat patch. The patch told Toole that the captain had served with the Special Forces in Vietnam. "Lieutenant tells me you're thinking about OCS. Is that right, Toole?" He looked straight at Toole with a smile. He reached into his pocket and pulled out a pouch with a pipe and tobacco. He lit the pipe. "Go ahead and smoke, if you like." Toole lit up a cigarette from the pack in his pocket, exhaled, and waited. It occurred to him that he had never smoked in front of an officer before.

"Well, yes, sir. I'm thinking about it." Toole relaxed a bit as he smoked. "I'm kind of worried about the extra time on my commitment though."

"Toole, I gotta tell you. I went to OCS myself, after I'd lived in the barracks awhile. Got real tired of KP and sergeants jumping in my shit all the time. Best thing I ever did." He paused. "I'm thinkin' you're the kind of guy who would rather give the orders than take them. Am I right?"

"Well, sir, I'd have to agree with that." Toole was smiling now. He liked the idea of palling around with officers or at least not being afraid of them. There was something comfortable about this conversation, and Toole hadn't been comfortable in a very long time. He let himself relax, his shoulders hitting the back of the chair.

"OCS ain't easy, you know. You're gonna have to earn that commission. Bein' an infantry officer is the most important job in the army. You think you're up to the challenge?" A challenge! Toole hadn't been challenged since he played college ball, and he found he missed it. And like that, he took the bait, settled the hook deep in his lip, and waited for the captain to pull him in.

"I think I can do it, sir," he said, surprising himself. "I'd surely like the chance to find out."

And that is how Aloysius Toole found himself with his duffel bag and his overnight bag, a big envelope with his personnel file and orders, and some extra money in his pocket at the bus station at Fort Benning, Georgia in April 1968.

When he got out of the cab in front of the big gray building, pulled his gear out of the trunk, and paid the driver, Toole was tired and his mind wasn't working very well. He'd taken the bus from home in Ohio, and it had been a long ride. The bus had stopped at every town and city along the way—Cleveland, Pittsburg, Harrisburg, Philadelphia, Wilmington, DC, and a bunch of others as it headed into the South. He'd eaten apple pie and had a glass of milk at each stop. But the stations were seedy and the men's rooms all cruddy, with guys throwing up and eyeing him sideways. "There must be a shortage of light bulbs at Greyhound," he thought, because the stalls were dark and the waiting rooms all full of shadows and discarded newspapers. His green uniform was decidedly unpressed after nineteen hours in the back of the bus. His hair, although short, was a lot longer than the other soldiers he saw running past him toward the jump towers off to his right. These were big towers located in a field, with a paved running track around them. "Airborne" was stenciled on the towers, and guys were lined up at the bottom of each one, waiting to climb the stairs. At the top, there were sergeants in black T-shirts with jump wings on their swollen chests, screaming at troops who would hook themselves up to some wire and jump out of the window, yelling "Geronimo!" and "Airborne!" It was only ten o'clock, but it was already hot. "Better get inside," Toole thought, "before I melt. I'm gonna catch hell reporting in like this."

As he dragged his duffel bag up to one of the doors, a kid in civilian clothes, khaki pants, and a blue oxford button-down shirt came out of the barracks and looked at him. "You Toole?" he asked, eyeing Toole's nametag. "We've been waiting on you. Let me give you a hand." He was smiling as he grabbed up the duffel bag and slung it over his shoulder and started inside. This kid was small—shorter than Toole, who was six feet—but he was clearly in great shape. He had next to no hair on his head, certainly none on the sides of his scalp, and there wasn't an ounce of fat on him. "I'm Lieutenant Taylor," the kid said over his back. "I'm going to be your tactical officer. Let's get you set up." Toole was astounded. What was an officer doing carrying his bag? And so nice?

"Here we are." Taylor led him into a two-man room and threw his duffel bag on one of the bunks. There were two desks, two footlockers, and two regular-sized metal lockers. And the room was spotless. On the desks were books and field manuals, two pads of paper, and some pencils in rows. "Your bunk mate's not here yet, but we should see him later. There's a lot to learn here, Toole. Get some sleep, and then you can start studying those books. Good to get a heads up. Mess hall's downstairs; chow's at 1200 hours and 1700 hours." He paused and looked Toole up and down. "You gonna need a haircut tomorrow. Make sure you've got some fatigues ready and a pair of boots. You got any questions?"

Toole was still astounded and figured it was a good idea to keep his mouth shut. "No, sir. And thanks for the help."

"Not a problem, Toole. Welcome to the Home of the Infantry." He was gone, and Toole was asleep almost as soon as he had packed away all his gear and found a set of boots and fatigues to wear.

Years later, Toole would always think of his time at Fort Benning with irony. He spent more than half a year of his life in the clutches of the place and yet never went anywhere near it. All his waking and sleeping hours were restricted to the woods; the barracks; running on the airborne track; and looking over at the dilapidated barracks where the washouts were sent, within an hour of their dismissal, to await orders for Vietnam. It was a dark cocoon, a space capsule of sorts, with only one door out, and there was no time for anything but infantry training and leadership. Martin Luther King had been killed as Toole travelled to the place, and Bobby Kennedy was killed as he entered his final months. Kids of all colors were rioting all over the country, and Woodstock was happening on a hundred different weekends. Yet he was aware of none of this, because there were no radios, no newspapers, and especially no time to ponder these great events. There was only terror, and for Toole on some bad days, fear and loathing. Yet the irony remained. When he left the place, immaculate in a brand new green uniform with infantry brass, very shiny second lieutenant's bars, and a body that could pretty much do anything, he felt like he was in control of his destiny and able to accomplish whatever tasks life set before him. What lessons he learned were burned into him like cigarette butts on the palms of his hands—they were shocking, smelled bad, and left scars. And they lasted forever.

"Get your sorry ass out of that rack, candidate!" Someone was screaming at him, right in his ear, and it hurt. Toole jumped up, looked around in the dark, and tried to figure out where he was. The lights came on and he saw the kid, that lieutenant who had been nice enough to help him up the stairs, standing over him in starched fatigues and cordovan jump boots. There was a guy getting out of the other rack as well, reaching for his fatigue trousers and looking dazed. Taylor directed his attention to him. "See these patches...See these patches?" The other soldier's fatigue blouse had a combat patch and some other patch on the other shoulder. There were also staff sergeant stripes on the sleeves. "These don't count. Simply won't do!" Taylor was screaming like someone had called his mother a whore. "You wanna be enlisted, candidate? You think being a sergeant is what you wanna be? Well, we got an answer for that. Yes we do. All candidates who don't want to be officers can go across the street to the repl. depot and head on out. You're in OFFICER school now, candidate. Your prior life just doesn't matter!" The lieutenant grabbed the soldier's shirt and threw it to the floor. He ground it into the waxy shine. "Now let's get downstairs and do some infantry! NOW, candidate!" He marched out the door into the next room and started his harangue all over again.

"Appears the tac is not happy this morning," Toole's new roommate muttered. "We'll talk later; time to go!" He pulled on his boots and hit the hall running. Toole was right behind him.

They were in a formation in front of the barracks and standing at attention. It was dark and warm. None of the soldiers who had lined up with Toole had been able to get their uniforms on properly, and this incensed the tac officer. Taylor was strutting up and down the ranks, pulling out shirts that were half-tucked into pants, pulling at bootlaces that were not tied properly, and grabbing at the covers of men who had hastily put them on their heads. "See these? See these?" Nobody looked at the tac. They were all at the position of attention and knew not to avert their gaze from anywhere but the front. "These, candidates, are enlisted covers! They have enlisted crests and ranks from all over the army. They don't count. They don't count! Everything you were, everything you think you've accomplished in the past, don't matter anymore." The lieutenant was wearing a helmet liner that had "OCS Tactical Officer" painted on it. "Helmets is all that matters to infantrymen. If you aren't squared away, how do you expect your troops to be squared away? You got to run faster, sing louder, think clearer, and shoot better than those you lead! Otherwise," he said, putting his head down and looking at the tips of his boots as if he was saying a prayer, "you're gonna get people killed. You're gonna get people killed, and you won't be able to accomplish the mission!" He walked to the back of the formation and screamed, "Remember this, candidates! YOU ARE RESPONSIBLE FOR EVERYTHING YOUR TROOPS DO, OR FAIL TO DO! EVERYTHING!"

"He had a great command voice for such a little guy," Toole thought. "How's he do that?"

"So now we're gonna run. We're gonna run for fun and see who wants to be an officer—who wants to give orders and be in charge. Most of you are gonna quit, or I'm going to throw you out of here and send you to the repl. depot. Because you're gonna find out you're not officer material. A commission is something you've got to earn! Anybody want to quit?" It would not be the last time he asked that question.

"No, sir" the soldiers yelled.

"OK, follow me!" Taylor gave them some marching orders and off they went, running around the airborne track for three miles or so. Then, without stopping, he led them off the track and into a cosp of woods. There was a stream there—a bit of swamp water the soldiers couldn't really see, but could feel. "Get down!" Taylor screamed. They all got on their knees and crawled into the water, Taylor in front. "You are going to spend a lot of time in the mud, candidates. You better learn to love it!"

They crawled until they could see pink in the sky through the trees. Their hands were in the mud with their legs dangling behind them. He knew better, but Toole was sipping some of the muddy water as they crawled because he was sweating, his arms were aching, and he was having a hard time keeping up. At one point, Taylor stopped and told the men to gather around him. He sat on the bottom of the stream and looked, for all the misery, like he was having fun.

"Now we're going to learn a song, candidates. We're going to sing it in the chow line this morning and the company commander's going to wonder how you learned it so fast. You're going to sing it real loud every time I tell you to, and you're going to learn to love it!" He started to sing.

> Far across the Chattahoochee,
> To the Upatoi,
> Stands our old alma mater,
> Benning School for Boys.
> Onward ever, backward never,
> Faithfully, we strive.
> To the ports of embarkation,
> Follow me with pride!

Toole was used to this hazing and recognized it for what it was. In truth, it was not a whole lot different than reporting in for football practice his freshman year at Youngstown. There were the preening leaders, loud and acting incensed; the mind-numbing head games; and the physical pain. He'd been through some of this in basic training and had learned to take it all with a grain of salt. Still, if this was the first day, what was the rest of the time going to be like? Toole joined in with the rest of the men in his platoon and within a half an hour had the words down pretty good. And so they sat there singing in the filthy swamp water as the sun came up.

Something was wrong though. Toole was very aware over the course of the next months that he was lagging behind. He couldn't accomplish all the tasks set for him by Taylor and often had a hard time staying awake. In the chow line, for example, he would stand at parade rest and move up as each candidate was granted permission to enter the mess hall. When Taylor or some other tac would come down the line, he was always being pulled out and told to do push-ups, straighten out his uniform, and go to the back of the line. There was only an hour for everybody to get through the line, and Toole never made it inside—sometimes for dinner, but never for breakfast or lunch. His room was always a mess, too, and he received numerous demerits. On Sundays he would have to march back and forth on the macadam with his weapon, singing the song, and doing push-ups whenever an officer walked by. "You wanna quit yet?" Taylor would ask him, and Toole would answer, "Sir, no, sir. Candidate Toole loves it here, sir."

"Well, then start acting like it!" Taylor would get in his face and scream. "Toole, I'm watching you. Seems you've got other things on your mind. You sure you don't want to quit and go home. See your mom? Get some sleep?"

"Sir, no, sir."

But after a while, Toole wasn't really sure. There were nights when, during the three or four hours he was permitted to sleep, Toole would dream about sleeping. He could actually see himself, having eaten his mother's pot roast, lying down and sleeping long hours. Waking up, taking a piss, and then sleeping some more. Other nights, he would dream about being in a jungle, leading his men into an ambush, and getting them killed. They were always in the swamp, and the blood coming from the heads and arms of his men would bleed out into the muddy water and all over him. There was always a lot of noise, and he wouldn't know what to do. The song was always there, along with Taylor screaming, "YOU ARE RESPONSIBLE FOR EVERYTHING YOUR TROOPS DO OR FAIL TO DO!"

He would wake startled and walk down to the head and smoke a cigarette, blowing the smoke out the little window in the shower. Maybe he wasn't officer material, like Taylor said. Maybe he should give it up, head to the repl. depot and let them take him. But there never seemed to be time to figure it all out, so he kept going.

The worst, though, was that his fellow platoon members were beginning to shy away from him. All the hours of the day and night were one big competition. They had started with two hundred and fifty candidates, and now over a hundred or so were gone. Everyone knew that the number had to get down to one hundred or so; there were a lot more that would disappear before graduation. And everybody wanted to make sure he was not one of them. If a guy began to straggle, couldn't do what was asked of him, was too tired to sing, his feet were too screwed up to run, his mind too weary to pay attention to all the details—he would be identified and ultimately killed. Too many demerits, too many walks on the macadam, too many times being pulled out of the chow line, and you could be the one. And Toole knew he was getting close. They said this was a team effort, but really everyone was on his own...on his own and alone.

Every month, they put the platoon in a room with forms and pencils on the desks. Taylor would tell them that they had to rate each other and turn in the forms. "Think to yourself, you are an infantry platoon leader in combat. Who would you want in combat running the platoon on your left and right? Who do you trust and who don't you trust?" He would stare at them. "Remember, candidates. This is serious. People are going to die if you make a mistake. You are responsible for everything your troops do or fail to do!" The bottom two guys vanished right after the platoon left the room, and Toole was always surprised that he was not one of them. You could smell the fear in the room, each man sweating as he looked around at the others, and Toole often considered that if he was really honest with himself, he would write his own name in at the bottom. Quitting was bad enough, he thought, but getting axed by those around you would be the worst. He never put himself in at the bottom of the list, but he sure never rated himself at the top either. Sometimes he put his friend George at the bottom and told himself that it was the right thing to do—saving lives and all. But he knew better and hated himself each time. It was confusing. He just didn't seem to get it.

Toole got counseled a lot too. Taylor would bring him into his office, stand him at attention in front of his desk, and review all his demerit slips and evaluation reports. "Candidate Toole, you're just not making it here. You really want to be an officer?"

"Sir, yes, sir!" Toole would bellow reflexively.

"Well, frankly I doubt that. I doubt that very much. You're not showing much initiative—officer's got to have initiative—and I'm not real clear on your judgment. Good initiative and good judgment—that's what matters here." He stopped and thought for a while. "You sure you don't want to quit?" If Toole had learned nothing else in the five months he had been at Benning, it was the answer to that question. He never even thought about it.

"Sir, no, sir," he bellowed. "Candidate Toole does not want to quit… sir!" Taylor was looking at him hard. It felt like he was going to check a box, close a file, and send Toole on his way out of the building to the repl. depot. It felt like it was over—his shot at taking some sort of control over his life pissed away, never to be regained. Squandered. They both smelled the fear, the rancid stench of impending failure that hung in the air as Toole sweated through his fatigue shirt. A steady stream of sweat drizzled down the side of his face, all but closing his left eye. It began to hurt. Toole knew that if he wiped it away, even blinked, it was over. He set his mind and looked straight ahead. Taylor watched the sweat and waited for Toole to react. After close to a minute, Taylor sighed and muttered,

"Well, OK. But this is your last chance. This is what we're gonna do. I'm assigning you as the platoon sergeant of the platoon. Candidate Lucky is the platoon leader. You and he are responsible for everything the platoon does or fails to do for a week. Got that? They fuck up, you fuck up. They fuck up…You're gone. Got it?"

"Sir, yes, sir!" And that's how the last test began.

Lucky wasn't a bad guy. He was one of those kids who had graduated from college and assumed he was qualified to be an officer. He didn't know much about the army, but that never seemed to bother him. OCS was just another test, and he was good at tests. The idea of the repl. depot never entered his mind. It seemed like he was entitled to graduate, and everybody agreed. He was safe.

"Looks like you and me got one more box to check off before we're outta here," Lucky quipped as he and Toole carefully laid their helmets on the desk in the platoon leaders' office. "Platoon leader decides what we're gonna do, and the platoon sergeant makes it happen. That sound about right to you, Toole?" He and Lucky weren't very close. They were in different squads and never really had much to say to each other. Toole assumed that Lucky always rated him really low on the "Who would you want on your right and left in combat?" exercise, but Toole didn't hold it against him. The rat list was about survival—yours, and those you trusted. It could bleed you dry, but it wasn't personal. Unless you were at the bottom and then, of course, it was very personal. "I'm thinkin' we got to do something to demonstrate some initiative this week." Lucky smiled as he shined the top of his gleaming helmet liner with his do-rag. "What do you think?"

That was Toole's problem. He never had a clue about what was appropriate in a given situation. You had to show some *initiative*— step out of line and demonstrate some distance between yourself and the herd. Show some *leadership*. But if you stepped too far out and things got screwed up, that would get listed as *poor judgment*, and you would get dinged for sure. Toole knew he didn't have too many dings left—none, really. He also knew that at the end of the week, he would be evaluating Lucky, and Lucky would be writing a report on him as well. Toole ventured a guess. "I'm thinking we take the platoon on a forced march in the middle of the night, out to the ranges, and when we come back as the sun is coming up, we get the platoon to sing real loud and wake up the rest of the company. I think Taylor would like that." Toole adjusted his gig line and looked at the floor.

"Yeah, that's a possibility." Lucky smiled. "But it's already been done. Nothin' new there. We got to show off some, show 'em we got balls...Have some fun. How's about a pogey party?" He started walking around the office, thinking it through. "Taylor's off on Saturday nights, right? So we call out for some pizza and beer, get us lots of chow, and have it all delivered to the barracks while he's gone. If we do it right, he won't see a thing; he'll hear about it through the grapevine, and we'll get points for taking care of the troops."

Toole was skeptical. Ordering food of any kind was illegal, against all kinds of regulations, and grounds for dismissal. Candidates ate in the mess hall, or they didn't eat at all. Keeping personal stuff in your lockers was also a huge taboo. During the first five months, the tactical officers checked the lockers almost every day and had dismissed candidates for just such conduct. But lately, they seemed to have loosened up a bit, with room inspections for sure, but rarely did they tell anyone to open his footlocker. Guys were sneaking candy into the barracks and consuming it fast, before the tacs came around. It seemed like the rules were slacking off a bit as they approached graduation. But it was hard to tell. Toole knew he had to look good to Lucky so he would write him a good evaluation. In the time it took him to dust the tips of his shined boots, he convinced himself a pogey party would probably work, and he committed. "Sounds like a plan."

And of course, it was easy. Everybody wanted to screw with the system, and they knew if they got caught, it would only be the chain of command, the platoon leader, the platoon sergeant, and the squad leaders who would catch any real hell. Toole set it all up, which, of course, was his job as the platoon sergeant. At lunch, while everybody else was eating, he called the pizza place. He got them to get some beer, and boxes of assorted candy and chocolate. He was getting into it when he ordered three bottles of schnapps and some Irish cream. On the sly, each member of the platoon paid his share. Toole was waiting in the boiler room when the pogey truck arrived and supervised his detail as they moved the food, beer, and liquor up the back stairs. Taylor was long gone, out the front door in civvies.

And what a party they had. Of course, Lucky was there to give it all out, being the platoon leader. But that seemed right as well. Lucky had decided the course of action, and Toole had made it happen. "Remember, guys," Lucky yelled down the hall, "all this crap's got to be outta here by twenty-three hundred hours! Don't want no evidence!" He laughed as he took a swig from the schnapps bottle. "Remember, this is all compliments of me and Toole here!"

At first, it was all good. A guy named Cricket was playing the harmonica, and a group of four guys was singing, "Where have all the flowers gone?" Toole's roommate was sitting in the corner, eating some pizza and drinking a beer; George was on a footlocker, drinking shots of schnapps and dancing like a hooker he was telling everyone about. Another guy, Boone, was smoking a cigar and telling stories about how screwed up Taylor was: "That little fuck will never make it in the woods!" And Lucky was back in his room, telling his boys how good it's gonna be when they were graduated. How much the ladies were going to love his tight lieutenant's ass.

Toole drank a couple of beers, but mostly he was watching out the window for Taylor. Around midnight, he told everybody that the party had to end. Nobody was listening. Toole went into Lucky's room for some help, but Lucky was passed out in his rack, the schnapps bottle wrapped around his hand. So it was up to Toole. He started yelling, screaming really, at the drunks, and they finally grabbed up their shit and put it in the garbage bags Toole had set about the hallway. By zero one hundred, everybody was snoring in their bunks, and Toole dragged the last bag down to the dumpster. "You throw a good party," his roommate mumbled as Toole hit his bunk. "Hope it works out for you." Toole fell asleep almost immediately. He had some Tootsie Rolls under his pillow and a Butterfinger in his spare pair of boots; but mostly, he thought, he had beaten the system and made it, with the good recommendation, to graduation.

Within an hour, the world came crashing down on him and the terror came back. Sure, Taylor was a bit drunk, but he was still in charge, and the party had wakened a righteous anger in him. It was a personal insult, something that required the infliction of pain, and Taylor was good at that.

"Ged up!" Taylor was screaming. "You fuckers get up 'n' stand on your lockers! Do it now or you're in the repl. depot and sweatin' bullets in Vietnam. Now, candidates…now!" The platoon was slow to get into the hallway—too much food and beer. They hated the idea of moving their lockers over the spit-shined floors, ruining the gloss that that had taken them five months to create. And they were scared, literally to death, at Taylor's power to change them from future lieutenants into privates spitting bad water and bad blood in some ditch.

Taylor had everybody stand on top of their lockers along the hallway in their skivvies. They were at the position of attention as Taylor walked up and down the hallway, bellowing with that great command voice of his. "Open up that locker, Candidate Cricket, and get outta the way!" Cricket jumped off his locker and tripped on his way down to the ground. "Had a little beer, did you, Cricket, and some pizza? What did you save for me?" Cricket opened the locker, and there were packages of chocolate, three cans of Coke, and what looked like a hot dog hidden under his shorts and socks. "Nice," Taylor growled, spittle coming out of his mouth and spraying over Cricket's face as he yelled at him. "You about the dumbest candidate at Fort Benning. I'm sure Toole here and Lucky told you to get this crap out of the barracks last night, didn't they?"

Cricket screamed, as loud as he could, "Sir, yes, sir!"

"Get that garbage can there and put all your crap in it. Gather up everyone else's while you're at it." And down the rows they went. Each candidate, except Toole's roommate, had piles of candy; pizza; a beer or a can of soda; chocolate and butterfingers; and chewing tobacco and cigars. George had a half bottle of schnapps and some pizza he was planning to eat for breakfast. The can filled up fast, and Cricket went to fill up another one. "You see here, candidates, your platoon leader and platoon sergeant tried to do something nice for you. They told you to disappear all this crap, but you didn't. Instead you screwed them. You might as well have put a gun to their heads and fired off a round. You candidates have no integrity. You can't be trusted. You aren't leaders. You are maggots. A leader has to be able to take orders as well as give them. You will kill people in Vietnam—your own people. You disgust me!"

It was 0400 by the time he got done inspecting everybody's locker and filling the garbage cans. "Cricket, take the cans down to my office. You maggots get dressed and form up outside my window. Lucky and Toole, report to my office now! It's time to pay. This isn't some kind of frat party," he muttered. "This is war. Move!"

In the dark outside, the platoon formed up, and Taylor screamed at them through the window. "Start with push-ups, gentlemen. When I blow this whistle, turn over and continue with sit-ups. Next whistle, you will get up and do thrusts. Next whistle, we start again." He blew the whistle and looked out the window to make sure they were on the ground. "Count 'em out, you untrustworthy maggots, count 'em out!"

He looked at Lucky, who was standing at attention in front of his desk. "What are you responsible for, Candidate Lucky?" Lucky knew the answer and belted it out. "Sir, Candidate Lucky is responsible for everything his troops do or fail to do, sir!"

"How about you, Toole?" Taylor blew his whistle and yelled out the window, "On your backs…Count 'em out!"

"Sir, Candidate Toole is personally responsible for everything his troops do or fail to do, sir."

"You start running in place." He reached over and grabbed a cold hot dog and a can of beer from the garbage cans. "Start eating, gentlemen." Lucky took the hot dog and put it in his mouth as he began running. "Toole, have some beer and some chocolate. You're troops saved it for you." Toole stopped running and popped open the can of warm beer. "Don't you think about stopping, Toole. You're going to run until all this is gone. Get to work!"

At zero five hundred, nothing had changed. Toole and Lucky were running and eating, the platoon was changing their exercises each time the whistle blew, and everyone was sweating. It had been a long hour, and Toole wasn't really sure how much longer he could go. They were about done with one garbage can, but then there was the other. If they failed to make it all disappear, they were gone for sure. And gone was beginning to feel like the only way out. "Toole," Taylor said, as he sat back in his chair and lit a cigarette, "you learn anything tonight?" He blew his whistle and watched as the platoon started to do push-ups. "Off your bellies, you untrustworthy maggots. Knock 'em out!" Toole grabbed a package of Butterfingers and began stuffing them in his mouth. He was sweating from all the running, and his stomach was really sour. "Keep eatin', Lucky; you can't let your platoon sergeant do all the work for you. You sorry maggot; you were in charge tonight. Now eat!" Lucky reached into the pail and retrieved another hot dog. He pushed part of it into his mouth and then bent over.

"Oh, Christ!" he muttered, and threw up into the pail. He retched two times.

"Keep running, Candidate Lucky, you're not even close to finishing what you started!" Taylor blew his whistle again. "You're the kind of guy who kills people, Lucky. You're a pissant little frat boy with an attitude. You better hope I kill you tonight, or your troops will do it down the road. Eat some of that puke. Don't leave it all for Toole here." He blew the whistle again. "So what do you have to say for yourself, Toole? You think you're a leader of men?"

Toole was sweating in streams, even though he was running in place and inside. It had been an hour or so, and he was getting dreamy. "I'm learning a lot tonight, Lieutenant Taylor. Can't trust troops, even when they are smart and know better." He reached over the pail and threw up. His stomach was convulsing, and he couldn't make it stop.

But he knew that if he gave up, threw the last chocolate bar down, and walked away from the puke and the sweat and the fear, it was all over.

"You wanna quit yet, Toole? Either of you fuck-ups want to walk away and give the platoon the rest of the morning off?" He blew the whistle again and watched the sun come up over the compound, as the platoon continued to do sit-ups. They were beat for sure. Some had stopped and were moaning on the ground. It reminded Toole of those 101st guys, waiting to get on the busses and crying for help. Toole was not sure what to say. Lucky, though, was getting a second wind as he got angry.

"Lovin' it, Taylor." He grabbed another chocolate bar and crammed it in his mouth. Then he puked it out again. "Lovin' it! Ah, fuck!"

"Sir," Toole mumbled as he grabbed a piece of pizza with some puke on it, "if you let the platoon go, I'll do all the drills you want. I ain't givin' up, but I'll do all the shit you want to give me." He wasn't thinking very clearly, but it seemed like a way out. That stopped Taylor in his tracks. He lit another cigarette and looked out the window. The platoon had been doing grass drills for two hours now. Most were faking it, and heat exhaustion was beginning to take over. "You two, outside. Bring the pail with you!" Taylor threw his cigarette butt in the garbage can and walked outside.

The sun was up now, and the August heat was beginning to get oppressive. "On your feet," Taylor screamed. "Look what you have done to your leadership." Lucky stumbled out first, sopping wet with sweat. He had puke up and down his shirt, and he looked like he might pass out. Toole followed and puked immediately on the stairs. "Keep running, you untrustworthy maggots. Toole, go throw up in the ditch." He pointed at the slow pool of water that ran from a drain from the building down toward the street. Cricket, go get us some ponchos!" Cricket was gone and soon returned with two plastic ponchos. "Put 'em on, leadership!" Taylor yelled. "Keep running, you lazy sonsabitches, and watch what it means to be responsible for troops! Now, candidates Lucky and Toole are going to demonstrate what it means to be leaders, what the price of leadership is. Platoon can sit now. I mean it. Sit the fuck down! You two, finish up that pail. Eat all that crap. Do it!"

Toole grabbed a Coke and opened it, although it was hot and hurt his stomach when it went down. He puked it up almost immediately. Lucky stared at Taylor but then took a piece of pizza into his mouth. "Push-ups, gentlemen—push-ups and then more crap, and then push-ups again. Now!" The ponchos only made things hotter. It was sweltering, and the ponchos made it seem twenty degrees worse as they landed in the pool of water and tried to keep the food down. Both wretched as they pushed their arms up and down, the puke landing on the sides of their faces and dripping off the sweat that was pouring from their bodies. "Some chocolate and then some sit-ups. Go!"

It was close to 0730 when Taylor seemed to get tired. Some of the other platoons were coming out of the barracks on their way to church and maybe some beers at the Candidates Club, and they watched in horror as Taylor wandered up and down the trench, supervising Toole's and Lucky's pain. They kept moving though. Nobody wanted to be in the middle of the shit-storm that was occurring around the trench. Toole and Lucky had puked multiple times as they tried to finish the garbage in the pail. They worked at the sit-ups even as the food kept coming up, and the platoon looked on, some even cheering under their breath. This was clearly out of hand, and everybody knew it.

"Seems you like cigars." Taylor dug around in the pail. "You like 'em so much, let's light 'em up! Leadership, get under those ponchos. Low-crawl down that trench, and light those cigars up. Get moving!" Lucky puked one more time and then got under his poncho. He and Toole low-crawled through the mud in the ditch down to the end and waited. The ponchos made it hot, and the puke on their shirts made it hard to breathe. Lucky threw up again, lifting up a side of the plastic poncho. Bits and pieces of puke were coming out his nose now, and he paused to blow it out and wipe it all on his T-shirt. The platoon groaned. "OK, Cricket, give them the cigars and a light. They're so good, your leadership can't wait to smoke them."

Toole could see a change in Lucky as they both took the lit cigars from Cricket and pulled the ponchos over their heads. He was white, bleach white, and draining every bit of confidence he had in him. Like a drowning man he went, holding the smoking cigar between his lips and getting ready to puke again. The last thing Toole saw, as he went under the poncho, was Lucky crying, or maybe just tearing from the smoke. Lucky was pissed, though, that was for sure. Toole went under, into the black, and looked for a place to release the smoke.

But Taylor wasn't done. "Low-crawl it, leadership! Low-crawl your sorry asses down the end of that trench. When you get back, we got more to drink, more to smoke, 'n' more shit to eat. See this?" Taylor was yelling at the rest of the platoon. "This is what happens when you fuck up. Fuck up 'n' people die. Your people! You kill people when you fuck up!" Taylor was crazed, screaming like some kind of evangelical preacher, and nobody knew where it was going to end. He ran down to the end of the ditch where Toole and Lucky were spread out, sucking up sewer water and waiting for the next attack. He kicked Lucky in the back, pushing his face into the sewage.

"Don' slow down!" Taylor screamed. "Lucky, I got a Baby Ruth for you!" He reached under the poncho and tried to stuff it in Lucky's mouth. But Lucky had had enough. The poncho came up over his head, and Lucky came out screaming, both fists flailing.

"I'm gonna kill you, you little fuck. I'm gonna kill you!" And out he came. Piss and puke, tobacco and smoke all over him, puke on his T-shirt and in his hair. His eyes were blurry from the smoke and his nose clogged up from bits of pizza lodged there from all the puking.

He hit Taylor, a good one close to his chin, before he fell on his knees, and then he pretty much passed out. Taylor went down in the mud but recovered quickly. He stood up, squared his shoulders, and looked down at Lucky at his feet. "*Remember* this, candidates." He had his dignity back. After all, he was an officer, and an infantry officer at that. He looked down at Lucky and waited a long two minutes. "Lucky, get up...You're done here. The rest of you recover and get back to the barracks. Platoon inspection in one hour!" Nobody moved for a moment; the idea of a candidate actually hitting a tactical officer had never occurred to anyone. And Lucky. He was a shoo-in for a commission…a real officer type.

Soon enough, though, they were gone. Back to their rooms, the barracks, to clean up the chaos all this had caused and get ready for the next exercise.

Lucky kind of woke up, and said, "Fuck you." Taylor, though, was through. He told Lucky to report to the repl. depot, and then he looked at Toole. "Come over here!" Toole couldn't stand up and kind of low-crawled on his knees and elbows over to where Taylor was, sitting on the stairs that led to the barracks, lighting a cigarette and then drinking a cup of coffee Cricket had gotten him.

"Toole…I'm gonna keep you. I'm probably gonna' get sent overseas for this little exercise, but frankly I've been waitin' to go for some time. I think you got the message. Maybe we serve together, heh? Remember, if somebody dies, and they're dyin' everyday, it's your fault. *Remember* this little drill—ain't nothin' to what we're gonna' have to do in the Nam." He got up slowly and walked away back into the barracks. Toole was the last man standing. He threw up once more, bent over as his stomach contracted. He grabbed up the ponchos, garbage cans, and torn candy wrappers and threw them in the dumpster. Then he struggled to stand upright and made it to the door. When he was finished, it looked like nothing had ever happened.

The rest was easy. Taylor was transferred almost as fast as Lucky, but of course Taylor went to some officer place, and Lucky went to the repl. depot. Toole saw Lucky once. He had sergeant's stripes on, but he was very drunk, telling stories at the EM club and too embarrassed to come out and see Toole. He vanished shortly thereafter, like the others, and the platoon moved on.

And then there was graduation, in bright shiny green uniforms, with national defense ribbons, gold second lieutenant's bars, and infantry brass. Bags were packed, and nobody was looking back. Toole said goodbye to George and his roommate, but there wasn't much else to do before he hit the bus station, with everybody saying they would meet again in Vietnam. Toole felt pretty good about getting through, but mostly he was relieved. He'd dodged a bullet, he thought. He was tired and leery. There was a little bit of Taylor on his shoulder and would remain there for years to come. But mostly, Toole knew he was on his own.

"Grazing in the Grass" was blaring from some boom box behind the small group of Quonset huts that passed for a PX in Di An, a fire support base in South Vietnam. Toole was walking up the gravel road that led from the perimeter to the middle of the base, and he suddenly realized how bone-tired he was. He had been in country for four months and had been out of the field on only two occasions. Otherwise, he had spent his time in the woods, on a small company perimeter or in the bush ambushing each night and sleeping in the rain. Two of his people had been killed stepping on booby traps and one more had burnt up from heat exhaustion—dying, and then dead as the platoon poured what was left of their canteens on his head. Otherwise, Toole hadn't really fired his weapon and had only been shot at once. Yet he was tired and weary, a bit hungover from last night's beer and pretzels at the officer's Quonset hut. He was stumbling, one foot in front of the other, toward a cold Coke and maybe some air conditioning. It was hot, even though he wasn't wearing a pack and all the crap he carried with him in the bush. It was dusty, and his nostrils were full of the thin red dirt that seemed to blow in spite of the windless, cloudless day. Toole thought about sitting down and just letting the war go on without him, sleeping some right there in the dirt. He was sweating through his fatigues and hoped it would rain. He accepted the one real truth of it all: *the only way to get home, to get out of the woods and the heat, the only way to find out if there was going to be a life after the Nam, was to keep walking.*

An infantryman's truth. And so he wiped his head with a green-issue kerchief and kept on walking.

Besides, he had a long list of stuff to buy for his platoon: toothpaste, razor blades, rubbers for the weapons, and a couple of cases of Coke, plus some cigars for his platoon sergeant. He also knew he had to get back to the company area and talk to the new meat—new lieutenants assigned to the unit—and give them an orientation and then, tomorrow, take them on the chopper to the field. The music changed to the Animals—"We gotta get outta this place"—as he made it to the nearest tin hut and walked inside.

Toole had taken a shower, but the water was hot pouring through a canvas bag a foot above him, and he continued to sweat as he tried to dry himself off. It was always better to take a shower in the morning when the sun hadn't boiled the water. But any shower was better than no shower, so he shaved and put on a set of jungle fatigues, which were all starched but had no rank or name tags on them; generic, he thought, like him. They were baggy, and he skipped the blouse and boots. His dog tags bounced along his green T-shirt as he plopped his boonie hat on his head, put his feet in a pair of plastic flip-flops, and walked to the back of the first sergeant's Quonset hut for a beer.

Seated on a wooden picnic table were two lieutenants, still wearing new fatigues with rank and name tags. A guy named Castle, all white and nervous looking, sat on the edge of the table, sipping a Coke and eating a steak from a paper plate that came from a grill that was sizzling meat off to the side of the area. There weren't any trees in Di An, but there was a corrugated tin roof over the two tables. The flies were bad, but the beer was cold and the scene kind of comfortable, as Toole contemplated the sun going down and the fact that he could relax a bit. Nobody would be hunting him tonight. He settled himself on the other end of the table and watched a line of soldiers with packs, M16s, thump guns and M60 machine guns, grenades, and helmets heading off to the line to stand guard for the night at the perimeter. Another guy, a short little sonofabitch with first lieutenant bars on, jumped off the picnic table and walked, like he owned the place, to the cooler where the beer was. "Way too much energy," Toole thought. "What's a first lieutenant doing in the land of butter bars and new boots?"

The first sergeant walked out of the back of the Charlie Company hootch, went to the cooler, and took out a can of beer. He reached to the table and opened a large jar full of cucumbers, vinegar, and peppers; closed the jar up; and stuffed the oversized pickle in his mouth. It made him sweat as the vinegar and pepper hit his mouth, and his eyes started to tear. "Damn!" he proclaimed. "They're jus' about done!" He popped the top off his beer, drained it in one chug, reached for another beer, and then his large black body seemed to convulse from his toes right up to his head. "Damn, tha's good!" he exclaimed.

Toole knew the first sergeant was one of those guys you didn't fuck with. The company commander didn't make a move without him—he was older than dirt, and he had been in the Korean War. He had a star on his Combat Infantrymen's Badge; this was his third time in Vietnam, and if he called you "sir" at all, you knew he didn't mean it. For Toole, he was just another stream to cross, another ambush to pull. Just another mountain to climb on his way out of here. "Heh, Top," Toole said. ""Who we got here?"

The big black man turned around and acknowledged Toole as he popped the second beer. "Well, Lieutenant Toole, this here's Lieutenant Castle, straight from Fort Benning, 'n' then there's First Lieutenant Coyle, all the way from Stuttgart, Germany, where he thought he was gonna' ride out the war without gettin' too dirty. They waitin' for your briefin'." He turned around and looked at a kid in shorts and flip-flops. "Rat! Bring me in one of them steaks." Then he went back inside.

"How goes it?" Toole asked as he reached for a beer in the steel cooler. "Where you guys from?" Standard stuff. Castle, it turned out, was from California, an ROTC guy from some state school out there. He was nervous, for sure, and kept looking over Toole's shoulder down the trail to where the fire support base ended at the perimeter line, and Charlie country began. Not much to see, but he didn't know that.

Coyle was a different animal. Short and squat, he was muscled but appeared to have some baby fat on him. Toole guessed it was from all the beer in Germany and being in the cold. Coyle was from Pennsylvania, had played college ball at some college in upstate New York and then quit, gone in the army, went to OCS, won the lottery to Germany, and then in his last six months got sent to Vietnam. "Who'd you piss off?" Toole asked. He'd never heard of somebody being sent to the Nam with only six months left.

"Someday, mebbe I'll share that bit of information," Coyle muttered. "But for now..." Coyle jumped up and got himself another beer. He grabbed one for Toole as well; ignored Castle, who wasn't drinking anyway; and jumped back on the table. "What you got to tell us about how to stay alive here?"

Toole explained all about how the company worked—how the company commander stayed in the perimeter and let the lieutenants run the platoons in the bush. He told him most of the guys were drafted, and there weren't too many senior sergeants around, so's you were pretty much on your own. He doubted that he and Coyle would see much of each other, since the platoons operated in different areas and were rarely inside the small company base at the same time. "Mostly we got VC hereabouts," he noted. "So far they seem happy to hide out in the bush, steal shit from the villagers, 'n' set up booby traps for us when we're patrollin'." He paused and got himself another beer. "It's a big fuckin' game. Not sure who's winnin', but it makes the time go by."

Coyle listened intently. "We're a long way from OCS," he muttered. They spent the rest of the night telling football stories before they collapsed on cots in the back of the supply room. Next morning they were up and gone, watching Di An fade into the distance. Castle looked like he was going to shit himself as they grabbed for rings on the floor of the chopper when it banked left, then right, out into the woods.

After a month or so, Coyle and Toole met again. They found themselves inside the wire of the company perimeter on the same day, and the company commander told them to drop by the CP for lunch. It was raining now—raining day and night. Neither Coyle nor Toole wore ponchos as they walked to the captain's bunker. "Too late," Toole thought. "Too wet and no chance to get dry until the monsoon season ends. Just another stream to cross." Some guys were standing outside, naked with bars of soap, washing themselves down; others were filling sandbags and fixing the wire that defined the company position. Others still were sitting under makeshift poncho huts, washing socks, reading books, or just smoking. After they stopped by the mess hall, another tent with a guy grilling hamburgers and hot dogs, they settled down onto a wooden bench under the captain's tent next to his bunker. Seated beside Toole was the executive officer, a guy named Boyle, who was a first lieutenant and had a huge waxed moustache spread across his tanned face. "So how'd you get him?" Toole heard the captain ask as they all sat down.

"Not real hard," Boyle answered, as he splashed catsup on his hamburger. "We was waitin' close to an hour on that little path just past the village—you know, about three mikes south 'o here. Right next to the blue. Dumb shit was didi boppin' up the trail like he owned the place. He wasn't supposed to be out after dark, 'n' it was just gettin' that way. Hit 'em twice before he knew what was happenin'…Gook never had a chance." Boyle splashed some more catsup and relish, and began to eat.

"Well, when Castle wakes up, he'll be happy to hear we got some for him," the captain muttered into his burger. Castle had stepped on a booby trap the week before and had been medevac'd to the rear. Word was he had lost a foot and was still suffering a concussion.

Coyle looked over at Toole with a question mark on his face. Where was the discussion about killing friendlies versus bad guys? What was this guy, anyway…a farmer heading home for chow? A guy out setting up booby traps? Maybe just a guy who got a little drunk and forgot what time it was. Toole recognized Coyle's consternation but didn't say anything. "We're a long way from OCS," he remembered Coyle saying. He nodded and got up to throw his hamburger away. Catsup and Boyle's war story didn't seem to fit together.

Once the captain finished his burger, he lit a cigarette and looked at his lieutenants. "So I got some news for you studs." The captain was an ROTC guy from Notre Dame and liked to talk as if he were in a football game. He'd been to Vietnam once before in the bad old days and was just hanging out with the company to get his command time so he could get promoted. He wasn't a bad guy…Just not real interested in what was going on, having seen it all before.

"We're takin' the company north with the rest of the battalion. Up near the Cambodian border. Lots of hard ground and NVA. Gentlemen…It's a different ball game." He exhaled and looked at each of his lieutenants to see who blinked first. Nobody did.

"Captain." Coyle looked up from his half-eaten lunch. "I know I've only been here a month, but I'm thinkin' these kids ain't really trained for serious combat. I mean, this AO isn't exactly crawling with enemy lookin' to knock us off." Coyle didn't smoke, but he was known to suck on a Tiparillo from time to time. He took one out of a plastic bag in his side pocket and popped it in his mouth.

"Yeah, I'll give it to you that everybody's pretty lazy down here." The captain was looking around for the mess orderly to get him some coffee. No one appeared. "Like they say at Benning—it's your job to train 'em up. Not to question why, just to do or die." He waited a bit to let that guidance sink in. "I scheduled us for three days of training in Di An before we head out—time to recalibrate our weapons, get some new equipment, and dry our feet out. Make sure your radios are workin'—not a lot of troops between us and them out there." He lit another cigarette. "Once they get a little paranoid, the troop's'll be all right." Boyle went for coffee, and they all sat around smoking and drinking from paper cups.

"When we going, sir?" Toole asked, just before he left to go back to his area of the perimeter.

"Three, four days…Up to battalion." There wasn't anything else to say.

Back in Di An, all had gone pretty well. The troops were given clean uniforms, they got to recalibrate their weapons on a rifle range out near the perimeter, and there was plenty of chow and beer. The captain held an awards ceremony, and Boyle got an army commendation medal with a "V" device for valor, as a result of his having taken out the villager. Even Castle got an honorable mention and a Bronze Star for losing his foot. He, of course, was back in the world now, and more than a few troopers contemplated whether or not a foot was worth an early trip home. "Sure you got to hobble around the rest of your life," Toole heard one of his guys say, "but you don't have to go up north and hump the bush with no NVA."

At night there was lots of time off too. The captain would set up shop in the officer's Quonset hut and invite all the lieutenants to play poker with him. He was pretty good, and as the lieutenants got seriously drunk, he took all their money and sent them back to their bunks busted. Nobody seemed to mind, though, since they really didn't have anything else to do with the money, and they were going north anyway.

The last night, Coyle and Toole got a hold of a bottle of Jack Daniels and rather than share it around, they climbed up on top of the Quonset hut to watch the fireworks. There were artillery shells and flares firing off at one end of Di An, and every now and then somebody would get nervous and fire some rounds out into the dark. "Pretty good show tonight," Coyle noted, as he lit up his Tiparillo and leaned back on the roof. They settled down to watch it all, contemplating the vastness of the starry sky, the tracers that disappeared into inky darkness, and the quiet that seemed to exist on top of the hut in spite of it all. There was even a little breeze. The war seemed far away and, awash in the bourbon, they let themselves relax.

"So you never told me," Toole said, as he swigged from the bottle. "How'd you wind up over here for six months?" It was, for sure, a mystery. Nobody got sent to the war for only six months...ever. Coyle waited a long time and although Toole couldn't really see his face in the darkness, he knew that Coyle was struggling with the idea of telling the story. He relented, heaved a sigh, and stepped in.

"You remember all that shit at OCS about taking care of troops," he muttered, and took another swig from the bottle. Toole shuddered, remembering Taylor and the pain in his gut from puking up all that pogey in the trench outside the barracks.

"Yeh," he said. "I remember."

"Well, we had a bit of a situation in the barracks over there that I was unfortunate enough to get into. Some black kids in my platoon, including a guy named Bobby Purify, locked themselves into the day-room one night and wouldn't let anybody else in. Seems they was protesting their treatment by the first sergeant, who was a big old cracker from Georgia. He was always putting them on extra duty—extra KP and policing shit. I ignored it as long as I could, even when they tol' me about it, 'cause, you know, no way I'm getting in between the First Shirt and the troops. The CO didn't much care either and backed the first sergeant up one hundred percent. Course it was Saturday night, and everybody was drunk. This black guy from another company was over and convinced Purify and the others that they had rights—you know, they were entitled to be treated fairly by the first sergeant—and they wanted to let everybody know what was going on. Gimme that bottle."

Toole could see the scene. Southern culture and black pride were bumping up against each other a lot. The black kids didn't trust you because you were white; the white kids thought you were their ally somehow. Most folks, though, black and white, were just trying to stay out of it—let things slide and get home in one piece. That was especially true in the bush, where everybody needed each other and there wasn't much time for buttin' heads. In the rear though, the troops had a lot more time to read what was going on in the world; there was a lot more alcohol, a lot more dope, a lot more boredom, and everybody was sensitive…real sensitive.

"Jesus," Toole whispered. "What did you do?"

"Well…I come into all this around two thirty in the morning. Of course, I'd been out all night myself and was a bit drunk too. They called me and reported that my platoon, or at least part of it, was raisin' hell in the dayroom and I better get down there." There was a burst as some guy on the perimeter fired into the night. Nobody fired back, and it got quiet again. "When I show up, Purify is sittin' on the couch sippin' a beer and looking about as scared as he can be. The kid from the other platoon, Mr. 'We Got Rights' snuck out the window, and the other two guys are standing in the corner waiting to see what happens. Nobody says much, but they do let me inside. Purify's nineteen if he's a day, and from someplace outside of Atlanta, Georgia. He's one of those kids that does what he's told—you know, just a kid. So he never gives me any trouble. Mostly, he's looking to please and stay out of the way. But he knows he's in trouble and looks at me with a face that says I'm his last hope. Given where he comes from, he thinks he's going to jail for sure, and frankly, I'm thinking maybe he's right. 'You ready to get out of here, Bobby?' I asked him. 'Back to your bunk?' 'Sure, Lieutenant.' And he paused. 'This thing got way outta hand.'

"As I'm walkin' the three of them to the door, the MPs show up. You know, three big white guys with billy clubs and 45s. The first thing this one sonofabitch does is crack Purify over the head. 'Get on the ground!' he screams. "afore I beat the black outta all of yous!' He looks to beat me down as well, but stops. You could see it in his eyes—I'm white, a little bit older, and maybe I got some rank on him. 'Who you?' he asks, holding his billy club in the air like I'm next if I give him the wrong answer."

Coyle takes a long swig out of the bottle and swallows it in two gulps. "Damn, that shit is strong…Whoa! Well, Purify's laying on the ground, and he's bleedin' pretty bad. The other two guys got down fast before they got hit, and the dopey fuck with the billy club is lookin' at me like I'm next. 'I'm Lieutenant Coyle…These are my men and if you hit one of them again, I'm going to beat you silly till even your mother don't know who you are!' I tend to get real mouthy when I've had a few, and anyway, the guy really pissed me off. 'Now outta my way…These men are returning to their bunks.' I pick Purify up, and we're getting ready to head to the door when the sombitch hits Purify again. I said, 'Stay down!'

"That's when I lost it. Not sure why, but the idea of some cracker beatin' up on poor Purify, and I guess the idea of him messing with my platoon, didn't square. I tackled Mr. Billy Club and spread his nose all over his face before the first sergeant and the other two MPs pulled me off of him. Needless to say, that ended it. Purify got taken off to jail with the other guys; I was told to leave the barracks and report to the company commander the next morning.

"By lunch, I was sitting on a tarmac waiting for a chopper to Ramstein Air Force Base with a set of newly printed orders for Vietnam, the Republic of, and here I am." He thought for a while. "Guess it could have been worse. Purify got court-martialed, and the MP had some kind of nose surgery. All I got was a trip to the big muddy…Like the boys say…Don't mean nothin'.…Now gimme some more of that bottle."

Toole didn't know what to say. He handed the bottle to Coyle and muttered, "Good initiative, poor judgment, Candidate." Coyle stopped drinking for a moment and then burst out laughing, pouring bourbon all over his shirt. Between laughs he said, "You got that about right!" and continued to laugh. Toole took up the giggles and then the laughter, and then he found he couldn't stop. The two of them laughed for a good five minutes, a bellyache kind of laugh that had them screaming and crying, rolling around on the roof and kicking their sandals along the corrugated tin. They laughed until it hurt, and it occurred to Toole as they finally settled down, wiped the tears from their eyes, and got quiet again, that he hadn't laughed like that in a very long time.

The North, it turned out, was a good deal different than the swampy and populated area they had lived in down south. For one thing, the place was covered in jungle—dark, unforgiving jungle, with great trees and undergrowth all twisted together; rotting tree trunks; snakes; and other animals. Toole and his platoon sweated from the time they opened their eyes in the morning and cleared the scum off the rags they used to hide their faces from the mosquitos. It was like living in a spider's web, a cocoon where some great hairy animal was keeping you until he was ready to kill you for his dinner. The jungle was growing, even as the soldiers moved through it. The jungle was alive, watered by the monsoon that delivered rain to the tops of the trees and trickled down constantly day and night. And the jungle was in control; yet there was no air to breathe, no water to drink, and no hard ground to sit on. There were small trails made by the animals that inhabited the place, but they were owned by the enemy—full of booby traps and mines, Punji sticks and sinkholes. There was no sky, no stars at night, and seemingly no way to get in or out. Toole and his people walked to the side of the trails, chopping the brush with their machetes and bayonets. They would come upon base camps in the jungle, full of prepared fighting positions, camp kitchens, hospitals, and booby traps. They would search and burn these down, using grenades to blow up the improvised bombs, and smoke and tear gas and more grenades to destroy the tunnels that infested these places. Twice, soldiers stepped on the mines; the medics would gather around a broken leg or a twisted arm, stopping the blood, wrapping the ragged appendages, and sending what was left off in helicopters that would send ropes into the jungle to gather up the remains in metal baskets. Mostly the camps were empty, but it was clear the enemy was out there somewhere, moving just in front of the company, waiting for an opportunity to strike back. At night, after eight or ten hours of trudging through the brush—stopping, getting sniped at, and clearing areas large enough for the helicopters to drop water and C rations, malaria pills, and sometimes mail—they would spread out into a company perimeter. They would scratch away enough brush to dig foxholes, send out three-man listening posts even farther into the darkness, and settle down.

The soldiers did well during the daytime, but at night they suffered from the bad habits they had learned in the South. In the dark, the real you-can't-see-your hand-in-front-of-your-face dark, Toole would often catch his soldiers lighting a cigarette up under a poncho or standing up to take a piss. The point was to stay real quiet, so the NVA didn't know exactly where your hole was and take you out. There were times when Toole would wake up after an hour of catnapping, look down the line, and know that nobody in his platoon was awake; the two who were supposed to be sitting up outside their holes guarding the perimeter were sleeping for sure. He would listen for a burp, a fart, or some sound of a man rubbing his eyes, and hear nothing but animals moving in the trees. The thought of NVA sneaking up on his line and cutting somebody's throat terrorized him and made him want to puke; it made him shiver and sweat all at once. He would leave his hole—hoping no one would mistake him for an intruder and shoot him—and low-crawl down the line, wake up those who were sleeping, then return to his hole and nod off again. Toole spent his nights in one-hour intervals: sleep, terror, and trying to figure out how to keep people awake so nobody would get killed. But there were no answers.

One night, there was a good deal of commotion down the line where Coyle's people were. Coyle was standing up in the middle of his platoon's fighting positions, screaming out into the darkness. He had taken an entrenching tool and hit one of his men over his helmeted head. It made a huge noise that insulted the quiet and stopped the monkeys and other animals from moving around. Then, he started in. "You motherfuckers want to sleep?" He had a good command voice, Toole thought, like Taylor back in school. "You assholes want to die here in your holes? Good. Every night I find somebody asleep, I'm gonna' stand up and tell the gooks where you are. Make it easy for the little fuckers to come and get you. Guards guard, goddamn it; sleepers sleep! Take care of each other or I'm gonna start a firefight for sure! You don't think I'm serious, try me!" He sat down in his hole, and everything got quiet again. Of course, the next morning the captain chewed his ass out, but word was nobody slept on guard in Coyle's platoon ever again. Seems they were more scared of him than they were of the NVA. "Good initiative," Toole thought, but he didn't have the courage to try that stunt himself.

And then they came to the village. It was a small town of wooden hootches with some sort of stone police station in the middle of it, off a village square. There was even a church and a Buddhist temple of some kind. The place was surrounded by a brick wall and barbed wire, and there appeared to be tunnels running from inside the ville out into the fields. There was a small road leading into the bush, going nowhere. Cambodia and Laos, they guessed. But nowhere they wanted to go. It was peopled by a couple of thousand Vietnamese farmers who worked in cleared fields outside the village around a graveyard, and these were the first people Toole and the company had seen in days. Their job was to surround the village in a great circle and settle in.

"So here's the deal," the company commander said, as he went about the process of lighting a piece of plastic explosive under a C ration can of coffee in front of him. The C-4 flared, and the water started to boil almost immediately. "The battalion commander's coming in this morning with the supply chopper. He's going in there to talk to the mayor and look around. We know there's NVA in there, getting some R and R, so we're going to surround the place and see what happens. Delta Company's on the other side. We send in the recon platoon and wait to flush the little bastards." He spread some peanut butter on some crackers from his C ration box and leaned his back on his rucksack and a tree stump. His radio crackled next to him amid boxes of C rations, battery bags, and other crap that made up the command center. "Doc." He looked at a long-haired soldier sitting off to the side of the circle. "Check everybody out. If we've got some real hard cases, you can send them out on the chopper...but not too many. We're gonna be sitting here for a couple of days...There's some replacements coming in, some food and mail. We'll spread all that out before we settle down for the night and see what happens." He lit a cigarette. "Nighttime's when the shit is going to hit the fan, so have your guys dig good fighting positions, put out your flares and claymores, and stay awake." He looked directly at Coyle. "No bullshit tonight, Coyle. We're in serious mode now. We kill some dinks, clear this village, and we get outta here back to Di An." He looked into the faces of each of his lieutenants to see if everybody was listening. No comments. "First Sergeant." He looked at the big man who had come in on one of the first choppers of the day. "You spread the replacements out when they come in, and bust some balls. Tonight's for real." He pulled a paperback out of his ruck and commenced reading, signaling that the meeting was over.

Even before the battalion commander was set to arrive, things began to happen. Everybody was working at their fighting positions, laying out munitions and pulling pieces of tree trunks into place. Nobody was paying too much attention to the fact that the villagers hadn't gone out to the fields, just stayed in their hootches for the day. It started to rain, and the place got muddy real fast. Then it happened. Two NVA soldiers came out of a hole, which was situated right in between some fighting positions in Coyle's area, and started firing. They were running for the jungle, throwing grenades, and spraying the area with their weapons. Two of Coyle's guys went down immediately and started screaming for a medic. Other guys ran for their holes to get their weapons and started firing into the village and at the NVA soldiers. Two more guys got hit, probably by rounds that were crisscrossing the perimeter, and everybody was face-deep in the mud. The NVA made it into the woods, and the captain started yelling for the soldiers to stop firing. When it was over, there were four wounded troops, all screaming for medics. The first sergeant was up and screaming along the line. "OK, ladies, get outta them holes 'n' start lookin' for more tunnel entrances. You assholes are in some serious shit now! Start actin' like soldiers." He was walking along the line and grabbing up troops and putting them on their feet like they were puppets. "Battalion commander's gonna want a secure perimeter when he gets here." He stumbled over a mound of dirt and looked down. "Well, looky here! Everybody outta the way; fire in the hole!" He pulled a pin on a grenade, rolled it into a hole in the ground, and jumped behind a tree trunk. It blew a good deal of dirt and debris into the air. "No dinks commin' outta that one tonight," he muttered, and continued his inspection. "Where's the captain?" he yelled, for the whole company to hear. "Another good command voice," Toole thought, as he pulled himself up and started checking to see if all his troops were alive and well.

"Over here, Top," the long-haired medic yelled. "'Pears we got a problem." The first sergeant walked into the center of the perimeter and observed the medic kneeling over the captain, who was sprawled out in the mud bleeding from his head and left arm. The first sergeant took one look and mumbled, "Shee-it." He turned around and yelled into the perimeter. "Get me Lieutenant Coyle. Where's Coyle?" Coyle was on the far side of the perimeter but knew enough to walk real fast toward the big black man. When he arrived at the center and looked down, he stared for a moment and then rubbed the mud and rain off his face. He straightened his back and settled his helmet squarely on his head. "Sir," the first sergeant said to Coyle quietly, "looks like you the company commander now. May I suggest you get your platoon leaders together and tell 'em what to do? We may see some more gooks in the perimeter afore nightfall, 'n' frankly, your command is all fucked up." Coyle nodded and looked away. He surveyed the entire company as it struggled out of the mud. Soldiers were looking out of the perimeter, guns ready to fire. Some were pointing their weapons into the perimeter as well, and some were still hiding in the puddles. Everybody was staring around, dazed, and for a moment it seemed like there was no sound at all. The jungle, the NVA, the villagers—all the background noise of the war had stopped. Coyle heard it… "You are responsible for everything…" It was in his head, but he spoke quietly to himself, "Yeah, yeah…blah, blah, blah." He woke up and started yelling, "Get me the platoon leaders at the command post now! First Sergeant, get the platoon sergeants on the line, and let's get these fighting positions together. Top, I want you to create a roving patrol; take a couple of guys and inspect every foot of this area to make sure there's no more tunnels…" He thought some more. "Let's get some listening posts out, some guards, and some claymores out. I want this place secure, I mean real fucking secure, in ten minutes, or I'm gonna have somebody's ass!"

He looked at the captain, who was breathing but knocked out. "He gonna make it?" he asked the medic.

"Yeah, I think so. He's shocky, but nothin' too bad." The medic started screaming at the captain to wake up and began bandaging his head.

"RTO." He looked at Jones who ran the radio for the captain. "Get on the horn and let battalion know what is happening. Tell 'em we got five wounded, the CO is down, and I am in command. We need replacements, a medevac for all five, and an ammunition dump...all before the battalion commander gets here. Got that?"

Jones got real efficient. "Yes, sir."

Of course, it never stopped raining.

Before nightfall, Coyle had the perimeter locked down pretty good. The lieutenants had been briefed and had all given instructions to their people, but Toole noticed there wasn't much for him to do. Everybody was scared and got smart very quickly. Funny what a couple of gooks and some wounded troops could do to straighten everybody out. The medevacs came in and took out the wounded guys; other choppers arrived with ammunition and food. The battalion commander decided to wait until the next day to make his visit but spent a good deal of time on the horn with Coyle. And at the end of the day, six replacements showed up with the mail. The first sergeant met them at the landing zone out in one of the fields and brought them to Coyle in the center of the perimeter. "More lovers for the cause," the first sergeant announced, and sat down on the tree stump.

Coyle was operating on all cylinders now—checking logistics, getting reports from each of the platoons, making sure everybody had enough batteries, lining up artillery fire coordinates, and checking himself to make sure there weren't any more tunnels inside the perimeter. He got some mail but stuffed it in the cargo pocket of his pants. It was getting dark. He looked at the replacements and shrugged. They were new guys, all shiny and clean—new boots, new weapons, clean helmets and bayonets, and carrying more crap then they would ever need. All privates straight from the world, and all wary and nervous.

None had bags under their eyes, and each one watched Coyle like he was some kind of god. One even saluted.

"Listen up," Coyle said. "I'm your company commander. You're going to be in fighting positions in a little while. This is a dangerous place, and we expect some shit to come down tonight. Do what you're told, and you're going to do fine." It was almost dark. "First Sergeant, you and me are going to walk the line and inspect the fighting positions. Then I'm going to come back and brief these guys so they don't fuck up. Stay close, gentlemen. I'll give you the good poop when I get back." And off he went with the first sergeant right behind him.

By the time he got back, it was just about dark. The new boots were still at the command center, sitting on their helmets, smoking their last cigarettes before the start of the night. Coyle noticed them and swore. "Shit," he almost whispered, "I don't have time to brief you right now. It's dark and you got to get to the positions. Tomorrow, I'll give you a good class on how to act out here. First Sergeant, spread them out. Give Toole two of them. Now put out the butts and take off." He looked at one of the privates who was standing up, a tall kid with big white teeth and the fear of god all over his face. "Private, if you salute me one more time, we're gonna have trouble. Got it?"

The kid almost saluted anyway as he stood to attention and said, "Yes, sir!"

And they were gone.

When the firing started, Toole didn't know whether it was his guys or the bad guys. Then a flare popped, and Toole could see three NVA coming out of a hole fifty meters in front of his position. "Light 'em up," he screamed, and his machine gunner took them out. All three fell into the mud and lay quietly. Now every one was firing into the darkness, causing the flares to pop. Someone set off a claymore, and there were grenades getting thrown out in front of his position as well, but Toole couldn't see any more NVA. There was a good deal of light out front, but Toole couldn't see what was going on in the fighting positions on either side of him. "Cease fire!" he screamed. His voice cracked; it was high-pitched and nervous. "Only fire if you see something," he yelled again, and eventually the firing stopped. "Anybody hurt?" he questioned down the line. No response; everybody was hiding in the darkness. "I'm gonna take that as a negative!" Toole barked and settled back in.

The next time they heard firing, it was across the village where Delta Company was located. Toole's guys started firing again out into the darkness, but stopped after it was clear nobody was coming their way. Coyle talked to Toole on the radio. "Watch your fire discipline, Toole. We don't want to fire up your ammo all at once. Remember, man, every time you fire, you're letting the little people know where you are. Got it?" Toole noticed how calm Coyle was and marveled. Toole was seriously jumpy and reminded himself to stay cool and focused. He was in charge of his little patch of heaven, and he had to remember that. Toole forced himself to crawl from position to position, counting ammunition, grenades, and flares. He was happy that he had partnered his two replacements with more experienced people, and everybody seemed glad to hear his voice. "Stay cool, guys," he whispered, as he hit each position. "It's gonna be a long night. Next time I come back, I'll bring the beer." The joke always fell flat, but the guys seemed happy to know he was out and about. He couldn't see their faces, but at least they weren't shooting at him. And, of course, it was still raining, which made it difficult to hear movement to the front.

"Sun's comin' up in an hour or so, over," Coyle whispered into the radio. "Pay attention, Toole; last hour of the night is the time they like to attack. Got it? Over."

"Roger that, Charlie-Six, over." Toole had started to call Coyle by his rank during the night. It didn't seem right to call him Coyle now that he was the company commander. It occurred to him they were a long way from damn near everything that had gone on before the evening began.

"Charlie Six, out." And that's when the last act began. Firing started over in Delta Company, which was scary because their rounds and tracers came through the village and passed over the heads of Toole's platoon. Then there was firing down the line in one of the other platoons; a claymore went off, and then another one. Now everybody was firing up and down the line; rounds were hitting the stumps in front of the positions, and somewhere a bugle was blowing. Toole could see NVA running along the side of the village and some coming out of tunnels Toole didn't think were there. Toole wanted to dive deep into his hole and keep his head out of the way of all the bullets and shrapnel flying around. But he couldn't see what was going on, so he forced himself to look over the top and fire his weapon.

"Charlie Three, Charlie Three, this is Charlie Six...How we doin' down there? Over." There was Coyle, checking in with all his platoons from the center of the perimeter. Somebody had a mortar, and there were shells landing inside the perimeter.

Toole grabbed the phone and was happy to have an excuse to sit at the bottom of his hole in order to hear. "I think we're good here, Charlie Six...Things seem to be calming down, over." Gradually the firing stopped, even before Toole gave the word. Delta stopped; the other platoons stopped; and then, as the sun came up, Toole could see ten or so NVA lying in the mud in front of his platoon. Toole crawled to each of his positions and recorded that everybody was alive. "Get organized," he barked at each of them. "This may not be over yet." When he got back to his hole, Coyle was on the line.

"Toole, this is Coyle...Charlie Two is down. There's some more wounded down the line. Go see what's happening, over." Coyle sounded rattled.

Toole continued to crawl down the line. There was sporadic firing around the perimeter, and he didn't want to get shot. When he reached the other end of the line though, there were three guys standing up next to a foxhole and a fourth, a medic, was down inside the muddy hole. "Ah, fuck...Ah, fuck" he was screaming. "Get me a medevac— two wounded here. Get me one for the lieutenant too. Ah, fuck!" Some guy was calling it in. Toole looked over the edge of the hole and saw blood, lots of blood, and then bits of body—an arm laying in the mud and an ear off to the side.

"What the fuck happened?" Toole asked.

"What the fuck do you think happened?" the medic screeched. "These two new guys got in one hole. Looks like one of them pulled a pin on a grenade and never threw it out of the hole. The explosion took them and all their munitions with them. These fuckers are seriously dead!" The medic was crying, bawling really, as he picked up body parts and tried to put them in plastic bags. "Who taught these new guys how to throw a grenade, anyway? What the fuck!" That's when Coyle showed up.

"Oh, shit," he cried. He jumped in the hole and grabbed the torso of one of the bodies, lifting it out of the slime at the bottom. "Medevac is on the way," he mumbled. "Let's get them to the zone." Right then, the mortar started to fire again, and shells were landing around the perimeter, blowing up trees, and spreading hot metal into the air. Everybody but Coyle got back into the mud and started firing at the village. Coyle remained standing. He picked up the body and started running to the landing zone where he laid it on a pallet of C rations. Toole looked up from next to the hole where he was trying to find out where the mortar fire was coming from. He saw Coyle run back, grab up the second body, and run through the shells to the zone. "Oh, shit," was all that was coming out of his mouth. Right after, Delta got the mortar guy and all the firing stopped. The shit was finally over.

After that, things got easy. Delta went through the village and found a few more NVA who never made it to the landing zone. The battalion commander showed up and inspected the perimeter, which the first sergeant had pretty well cleaned up. The troops were eating breakfast from cans when the colonel came around and congratulated them on a job well done. The medevac had already come and gone, and the dead NVA were lined up in a row—all twelve of them on Charlie Company's side—so everybody could take a picture. Next thing Toole knew, Bravo company was coming into the landing zone, and his platoon was taken out, back to Di An. Everybody was pretty relieved to be alive, and the conventional wisdom was that if somebody had to die, it was best if it was the new guys since nobody knew them anyway. Indeed, given how late they had come in, it was like they were never really there at all. It stopped raining.

The word around the company was that Coyle was going to get a medal for carrying the two guys through the mortar fire to the landing zone. A new company commander had been assigned by then, and the first sergeant had things pretty well back to normal. Except that nobody could find Coyle.

"Where do you suppose he is, Top?" Toole was sitting in the company supply room, doing an inventory of the new guys' duffel bags so they could be sent home with a letter from the company commander.

"Last I heard," the first sergeant said, so the two supply clerks couldn't hear, "he stole a jeep from the motor pool and headed into the ville. He's probably drinkin' at the whorehouse I guess. Feelin' sorry for hisself 'bout gettin' those new boots kilt." Toole had pretty much come to the same conclusion.

"You think I should go get him?" Toole asked. It was illegal for officers to go to the whorehouse. Toole wasn't sure what to do.

"I'll tell you, Lieutenant. Iffen you don't, 'n' he don't show up to get his pretty medal, he's gonna be in a world of hurt." He stopped and considered whether or not to say anymore. "Lieutenant Toole, lissen here. What happened to Lieutenant Coyle sucks. A real fuck-up that none of us sat those kids down 'n' showed 'em how to fight in a foxhole. You 'n' I both know the lieutenant was pretty busy that night. Iffen he hadn't stood up 'n' straightened out the company 'for the gooks come a runnin'...Shit, we all be in bags waitin' to go home." The first sergeant reached into a mermac container and pulled out two cans of beer. He handed one to Toole. "Lieutenant, if Coyle's a friend of yours, you better go scarf him up 'for the MPs get him. Be a shame to see a good officer run over by the green machine. Hell," he said, as he cracked the can in two and threw it in a box in the corner, "there ain't that many good officers around. Shee-it." He shook his head and walked out of the Quonset hut.

When Toole pulled up to the whorehouse, he was seriously nervous. He had never been outside the wire before without a platoon of guys to protect him, and he didn't really trust the Vietnamese not to turn on him. He knew not all the Vietnamese were bad guys—that was pretty obvious from the way he had been treated in some of the villages his platoon had walked through in the first few months he was in-country. Problem was, you never knew who was who. One day you're playing with some kids, the next day there's a grenade in your pack. He took his M16 with him as he walked inside the two-story building, but it was early, and there didn't seem to be anyone around. He waited for his eyes to adjust to the darkness and then walked the perimeter of the building until he found Coyle passed out in a booth, his arm wrapped around a bottle of Jack Daniels. He had a .45 pistol in his other hand. "Heh, Coyle," Toole whispered and grabbed for the bottle, "time to wake up." Coyle jumped, held onto the bottle and stared at Toole, trying to figure out who he was. "It's Toole, man—Toole. I come to get you."

Coyle tried to take a lick off the bottle, but missed, and the bottle fell to the floor. "He's pretty fucked up," Toole thought.

"You talkin' to me?" Coyle was slurring his words. He wiped his eyes with his hands and noticed the .45 as it hit his forehead. "Oh, yeah." He brought the left hand down on the table. "You talkin' to me, Candidate?" The .45 was pointed at Toole across the table, and Toole instinctively moved to the right, out of its line of sight.

"You catch their names? You figure out who those little bastards were?" Toole knew who they were. Indeed, except for the first sergeant—who had to fill out the paperwork on dead and wounded, take them off the company morning report, and get the new company commander to sign the letter that was going to be sent home with their stuff—Toole was the only one in the company who did know their names. He'd done their inventories.

"Yeah...I know 'em." Toole paused and went silent.

"So who were they? I want to know their names. Especially that tall fucker who kept trying to salute me. Who were they?" Toole didn't see any point in going through all that again. He had rifled through their duffel bags, the place where soldiers kept their most intimate stuff—sometimes their only stuff—and the exercise had unsettled him. The one guy, Private Marley Pickens, was a nineteen-year-old recent high school graduate from Granville, Tennessee. He had a picture of himself in a tuxedo with a good-looking girl who had a "Belle of the Ball" sash draped over her gown. Toole had had to stifle the thought that he wouldn't mind meeting her someday. Seems Pickens was a baseball player, because there was a high school letter with a big "B" in the duffel bag. And there were letters all perfumed with hearts on them as well. Toole didn't read those. Pickens had a picture of his family too—a proud dad, an apprehensive mom, and two little brothers in front of a trailer park. "My family" was written on the back. "Sure do miss 'em." There was a set of khakis; an expert's marksmanship badge; a spit-shined set of black army shoes that were all moldy and cracked up; and a diploma from his basic training class at Fort Dix New Jersey, signed by some colonel six months earlier. Toole had struggled with the idea of sending the love letters to Pickens's mother, but thought they might be kind of intimate. To know, of course, he would have had to read the letters, which he really couldn't bring himself to do. He left them out of the packet and threw them away.

The other guy, Private Wilbur "Butch" Cassidy, didn't have much to inventory. His khaki uniform, of course; a small bag of marihuana and a pipe; and some playing cards. Seems Butch was a bit of a wild one. There was a shot of him with some training platoon in a bar in Columbus, Georgia, all beered up, and a picture of him outside a club in New York City with long hair, bell-bottom trousers, and a chick who looked like she might have been touring with some rock band. Not the lead singer; maybe a roadie. Old Butch had been the guy who kept saluting.

"A guy named Pickens and a guy named Cassidy," Toole responded. "Not much to say. Just some guys who made it to the big muddy and now they're going home." Toole paused. "Look, Coyle, we got to get you outta here. The MPs are gonna be by in a little while. First sergeant says if I get you back and sober you up, nothing's going to happen. Come on now, let's go."

"Pickens and Cassidy," Coyle muttered. "Pickens and Cassidy."

"Yeah," Toole answered. "Just some guys in the wrong place at the wrong time. We both know shit just happens sometimes," Toole trailed off. "Guess it just happened to them."

"Some guys!" Coyle was getting all excited. "Some guys? They were my guys, my troops!" He was heading back into his stupor. "My responsibility." He passed out on the table again and Toole watched him for a while. He thought about waiting for the MPs, who generally swept the place most mornings looking for drunks and awols. But that would result in Coyle's awol becoming official. The new company commander would have to take some action, and officers going awol rarely got a pass. Maybe he could carry him to his jeep and get somebody to come out and retrieve the one Coyle had stolen. The first sergeant could talk to the motor officer, and nobody would be the wiser. Of course everybody would know, but they could ignore it. Coyle could stand the formation, get his medal, and life would go on. That seemed like the thing to do, so Toole woke Coyle up—shook him up, really.

"We got to go now, Coyle. We got to get you back to the company and sober you up so's you can get your medal, and we can worry about the other shit later. Formation's at thirteen hundred hours. Come on now, Coyle, we got to go!" Toole was almost screaming, trying to get into Coyle's head and get him to focus. "Stand up, Candidate. Time to do some infantry!"

Coyle responded. He straightened his back and almost braced at the table. "Oh yeah...the medal. We got to go." He slid over to the side of the booth and stood up, his right hand on the table steadying him and left hand still holding the .45. "The medal," he said under his breath.

"Look, you go get the jeep; I'm gonna take care of some business in the head here and meet you outside. Candidate Toole, it's time to get the medal!" And off he staggered to the toilet in the back of the building.

Toole waited for him at the door. The sun was out, blaring, and it hurt his eyes. As he was putting on his sunglasses, he heard a shot from the back of the building and knew immediately to run after Coyle. "Oh no!" he screamed. "Oh, shit!" When he turned the corner, he saw Coyle slumped over the urinal, his head down deep in the drain, the .45 still in his hand. Coyle had clearly fired the weapon, and half his ear was splattered into the pisser. He was moaning; he was crying. Coyle was broke, but he was alive. Toole grabbed the weapon, cleared it, bent down, and pulled Coyle's head out of the urinal. "You dumb fuck!" he screamed. "You dumb fuck!" A mamasan came in, took one look, and started screaming.

"You fuckin' GIs! You fuckin' GIs!" Her voice was screechy but loud. Commanding. "MPs gonna come and close me down! You fuckin' GIs neva know when to quit. You fuckin' GIs!" She walked back into the bar area and sat down muttering. "Dinkydow, fuckin' GIs!"

In a way, it was all easy after that. The MPs did show up, and they took Coyle in their jeep back to Di An. He went directly to the hospital, and then he was medevac'd to Japan since his head wound was apparently serious but not life threatening. Of course, he was missing an ear, so he was going to be spending a lot of time in the hospital. Mostly in the world after they got him stabilized. Toole never saw him again.

They held the formation at 1300 hours. The battalion commander showed up and said some words about how Coyle had been wounded in action and had to be medivac'd. The lieutenant who had been wounded and the other guys who had been killed all got medals, although for some reason the colonel didn't get Picken's name right and kept calling him "Private Marley." Nobody but Toole and the first sergeant noticed.

Years later, when Toole would have a bad night—when it was raining and the sky would go inky black—he would think on Coyle. He thought about going to find him. He missed him; missed the great laugh on the tin roof and the sheer joy, albeit unstated and really un-recognized, of finding someone in all that emptiness—aloneness—who had shared all of that and who had understood him. But it wouldn't do, and Toole knew it. The whole thing had been shameful really. Young men trudging through a great play, doing their best, their bloody best, yet making huge mistakes that stopped other young men dead in their tracks. Taylor's great responsibility, impossible to carry—a large rock in a perpetual rucksack. Toole knew that what he really missed most was his youth and yet, he often mused, he was glad that it was over.

GIVING UP THE GHOST

It was time for him to go to bed. Long past time, if you counted the thousands of hours he had spent over the years avoiding the exercise—all the beer he had drunk, the shots he had put away, and the multiple books he had read. Even the impressive time he had spent on C-SPAN and with the old movies. He was now an expert in the minutiae of the American political process and capable of quoting numerous pundits who presumably slept the night away after venting their most terrible predictions for the future. By now, Michael's habit was to remain awake, lights on and TV blaring, until he fell into fits of exhaustion. A couple of hours here and then a couple of hours there, until the sun came up and he could direct himself toward the lists of tasks he made on his pad, operate on the adrenaline the tasks produced, and get through the day. He found he could catnap between the tasks, sleep in his car, lie down on a sofa in a crowd of people going through their day, or just stare out the window for a half hour or so. His friends said, "Michael can sleep anywhere," and yet getting into bed, pulling the cover over him, and waiting for his body to ease into rest was beyond him.

Now it was his habit to avoid his bed altogether; and so his nights were spent browned out, sputtering energy like light bulbs with broken filaments, like broken lines of half-finished poems and short stories. All in all, the packs of cigarettes smoked, the alcohol consumed, and the junk food stuffed into him were taking their toll. Day was becoming night and night day, a semiconscious set of movements he followed to keep the time going. He had been getting by, but the vague pain his body felt was catching up with the pain in his mind. He had to make a change or he would break. And so it was time for him to go to bed.

He wasn't really sure how it had all started, but he knew he couldn't stand being alone in the dark. Something to do with being on ambush, he supposed. The long nights in the rain pulling the hair on his arm to stay awake, listening for the sound of rocks turning over or the splash of puddles. Rarely did the little people come out of the dark, but when they came, they brought fire and terror, and bugles and fireworks so loud you wanted to get deep in a pool of water and wait for it all to go away. But, of course, if you did that, did what seemed appropriate, the other guys—Mitchell, Johnson, and Alphabet—would get surprised. And more than that, the little people might just sneak right up on them and cut their throats. Michael hadn't done much to be proud of since he got back, but he knew he'd never let those guys down; no gooks snuck up on him when he was on guard. Not even the one time when he had fallen asleep and woke up in a fit, shaking like he couldn't stop, scared almost to death that the little people were on him as he nodded off. They weren't there that night, but the thought of nodding off, even when it hit him in the daytime, would start him sweating and shaking again. After that, he had taken to spraying insect repellent on his balls to keep himself awake. Sure it brought him to tears each night, but it kept him awake and that was enough. He'd done his year without getting anyone personally killed. And that was enough. Some guys drank too much, other guys smoked too much dope; other guys popped pills or even used needles. For Michael, his habit was to stay alert; on guard; and present to smells and sounds, and even the lack of sounds, in the pitch. Knowing he was safe, but listening nonetheless.

A guy at the VA—a guy who was taking methadone to get off heroin and who had been to multiple meetings and counseling sessions, a guy who had been a helicopter pilot or some such thing—got ahold of him one day and told him something that stuck. "You got to try something different, bro. Like they allays tellin' us; what we're doin' ain't workin', so's we got to change the way we operate. Turn in our ol' habits for some new ones." This guy, Lucifer, bummed a cigarette and lit it with a Zippo lighter he kept in his fatigues pocket. "You ever try prayin'?" Praying. Michael had almost laughed in Lucifer's face, but he could see the guy was serious, at loose ends, and grasping for whatever worked.

"Prayin." Michael had mulled the word over and almost spit it out into the dirt. "I went to see the chaplain," Michael muttered. "He told me if I pray to god, eventually he would see fit to let me get some sleep." Michael exhaled, field-stripped his cigarette, and put the butt in his pocket. "Problem is, well, I'm not sure what I believe about god. Haven't seen him around much, you know?"

"Shee-it." Lucifer kind of smiled, a half-smile that drooped down the side of his face and stopped at the stubble that passed for his goatee. "It ain't never 'bout what god needs. It's about what *you* need. If prayin' to a fuckin' rock'll get you to give up that ghost you carryin' around, pray to a fuckin' rock, my brother. Pray to a fuckin' rock. Now gimme another cigarette. I got to wait in line for my methadone. Mebbe I'll see you tomorrow." Michael offered him the pack, and the guy took two cigarettes with another sort of smile. He wandered into the building without another word, sort of limping, his shoulders hunched over and his hands in his pockets.

That night, Michael went home and sat in front of his TV set, drinking a beer and eating a small pizza he had picked up on the way. He got his ashtray settled on the coffee table and started in on the news. "Got to do something else," he muttered. "Got to change the way we operate." He thought about Lucifer and wondered what his story was. Just another guy hanging out at the VA with nothing better to do and no place to go. "Seemed pretty smart for an addict though," he thought.

The pain started as it always did, telling him to lie down and get the weight off his feet. It moved up his legs and settled in the small of his back. There was the usual headache and tightness in his neck, and his eyes itched. He was weary—tired of the pizza, the beer, the cigarettes, and the news. Tired of staying up and tired of lying down. Tired of fighting. He was surprised to find himself standing up and walking into his bedroom, pushing the clothes off the bed, and stripping down to his shorts. He was even more surprised to find himself under the covers, his head resting on the pillow, and his legs stretched out straight. And he was even more surprised to find himself reaching over and turning off the light.

As he lay there, he could hear the plumbing—water trickling through a radiator somewhere in the house. He could hear the fan in the kitchen as it went through its rotations, and he could feel the darkness spread around him—a terrifying glue that wanted to suck the air out of his lungs and leave him for dead. He could smell the color of it all, taste the rust that was his life and the absence of any hope that anything would change.

And he prayed. He decided on the "Our Father," the one prayer he could remember the words to, a prayer he had said when he was small—when he could sleep. "Our father, who art in heaven, hallowed be thy name…" After a while, after maybe ten times through, the prayer got easier. He remembered saying it fast when he was young, not listening to the words or really thinking about what they meant. And he said it that way now. Fast, rote fast, over and over again, until it was a jumble of words, until the sounds disappeared and the pitch receded. He said it until the air moved easily through his nostrils and his lungs. He said it until he wasn't saying it out loud anymore, until his mind was working it over and over again by itself. And somewhere in the middle of the words, somewhere around "and deliver us from evil," he fell asleep.

The next morning, around ten o'clock, he woke with a start. It scared him some until he remembered where he was and how he had gotten into bed. His headache was still there, familiar but less severe than he was used to. There was a strangeness to how he felt, and he was wary as he walked into the kitchen for a cup of coffee. All the cricks weren't gone, and all the aches and pains hadn't magically disappeared, but he experienced for the first time in as long as he could remember an energy, a sense that maybe there was something new happening. "Could the ghost really be gone?" he thought.

After work, he went down to the VA to look up Lucifer and tell him what had happened. He stood in the portico of the building smoking a cigarette, hoping Lucifer would wander by, but he didn't. Michael went inside and found the methadone clinic. All the junkies were there waiting to get their medicine, leaning up against the walls in their jungle fatigues. The security guard was there, telling them they couldn't sit on the floor and that if they wanted to smoke they had to go outside. The guys were bitching to themselves because they wanted to smoke, but they didn't want to lose their place in line. Michael walked up to the men and stopped in front of some brothers who were bobbing and weaving, muttering to themselves. "Heh, any of you guys know a brother named Lucifer—comes down here to get his methadone about this time of day?" Michael asked. Two white guys with long hair and untrimmed beards looked away.

"You mean Lucifer the helicopter man?" One of the brothers asked, keeping his eye on the line so he wouldn't lose his place. "Lucifer gone, man...gone."

"What do you mean, gone?" Michael asked. "He's here every day. Where did he go?"

"I mean gone gone," the man said. "As in down for the count, took one for the team, eaten by the bear. Took-a-nap-and never-woke-up gone." He looked away and shuffled toward the dispensing window. "Gone."

And that was how it worked. For Michael, the ghost retreated from his bedroom each night as he said his prayer over and over again, and eventually he was able to sleep whole nights without waking up with a start and beginning the prayer over again. He learned to trust it. And he learned not to miss the weariness and the dull pain of fighting the darkness. With the energy came a small bit of hope that touched him all the rest of his days, even as he thought of Lucifer and prayed; his sleep was finally profound and sweet.

Richard Michael O'Meara is a retired soldier and trial attorney who lives with his wife, Mary, on an island in southern New Jersey.

Proof

Made in the USA
Charleston, SC
08 May 2015